Carving for Cara

A DARK ROMANCE HALLOWEEN NOVELLA

MELISSA MCSHERRY

DANA LEEANN

Carving for Cara

A DARK ROMANCE HALLOWEEN NOVELLA

MELISSA MCSHERRY

DANA LEEANN

TRIGGER WARNINGS:

YOUR MENTAL HEALTH MATTERS.
READ THIS PAGE IN ITS ENTIRETY.

This book contains(but not limited to) content depicting violence, gore, explicit language, knife play, consensual non-consensual sex, sexual assault, restriction, stalking, mutilation and death of a side character, praise, mention of addiction, marijuana use, gagging, excessive force, choking, and explicit sex scenes.

This book is not intended for readers under the age of 18. Read with caution. Your mental health matters.

The book you are about to read is DARK and not recommended for all readers. Read through the trigger warnings once more, then decide if you should continue on with this book. The content within this book is heavy.

Continue to next page...

TRIGGERS:

Violence, gore, explicit language, knife play, consensual non-consensual sex, sexual assault, restriction, stalking, mutilation and death of a side character, praise, mention of addiction, marijuana use, gagging, excessive force, choking, and explicit sex scenes

You have been warned.

PLAYLIST:

Nightmare - From Ashes to New

Villain Era - Bryce Savage

Breathe - Kansh

The Death of Peace of Mind - Bad Omens

Bow - Reyn Hartley

If I Didn't Know Better - Mack Loren

Dirtier Thoughts - Nation Haven

You Put a Spell on Me - Austin Giorgio

It Had To Be You (Dark Version) - Tiffany Ashton

Honey Catching Season - King Mala

In Bed With A Psycho - Layto Nameless, Stevie Howie

For the girls who dream of being chased through a cornfield by a masked man, then fucked in the pumpkin patch when he catches you

Chapter One
CARA

An icy breeze stings my pale, tattooed skin as I hold my favorite purple lighter inside the final unlit jack-o'-lantern showcased on my front porch. The tiny orange and blue flame dances in the wind, and I struggle to shield it from the brisk fall elements while I'm shoulder-deep inside this monstrous pumpkin.

Each year, I go all out for the spooky season, and this year is no exception. If anything, I've felt the spirit of Halloween even more than usual, and my house is decorated accordingly with six masterfully carved pumpkins poised atop my porch, numerous grungy gravestones strategically placed among overgrown blades of grass, and bright red lights that flash to a playlist I titled "Monster Jams." I've even got a dry ice machine blowing vapor through the yard. My neighbor hates it, but I don't give a fuck. He lets his dog shit on my grass every morning when they walk by, and not once has his lazy-ass bothered to clean it up. There will be a day I finally snap and leave a flaming bag of dog crap on his front steps, and I have a feeling it'll be sooner rather than later.

My modest Victorian-style home sits on the quiet corner of October Lane and Cemetery Circle. I was fortunate enough to buy it for next to nothing eight months ago. My income as a tattoo artist allowed me to wait it out in a rental studio while I watched it waste away on the market for nearly two years, dipping in price once every couple of months until I was finally able to afford it. The street names alone were enough to scare off half the buyers, and anyone else that remained wasn't looking for a gothic grey and black house to renovate into a cozy family home. Most people in my small town of Hallow Grove, Iowa, are superstitious and fearful of the devil, but after reading one too many dark romance novels, I'm reasonably certain he'd fuck like a god.

I flinch as my cell phone rings, aggressively vibrating in my back pocket as it begins to play a metal remix of "This is Halloween." Sucking in a deep breath, I wipe a stray strand of hair from my face and force myself to regroup.

My heart is thumping against my chest, and I hate that I'm feeling so on edge this evening. It's probably due to the drawn-out anticipation of seeing Jonah, my ex-boyfriend, at the Devil's Night party tonight.

He's a… complicatedly uncomplicated situation, so to speak.

We dated throughout high school and a few years after, but I eventually came to the realization that he was both manipulative and a liar. Some days he walked the line of being verbally abusive, but he never went as far as laying an ill-intended finger on me. After a few years apart with zero communication, we ran into each other at the corn roast festival last fall, and we've been hooking up ever since. There are zero feelings involved. It's just casual fucking when one of us wants it.

My phone continues buzzing, reminding me to slide it free from my tightly fitting jeans.

SLOAN pops up on the caller ID, accompanied by the most humorous picture of my best friend passed out drunk in my bathtub, and I smirk, quickly forgetting how anxious I've felt all day.

"I'm almost done lighting my pumpkins," I say as I bring the phone to my ear. "Are you leaving work?"

3

Sloan lets out a painfully slow and dramatic sigh on the other end of the line. "Yes, finally. I'll be at Rustic Roast in ten. I might die if I don't get a pumpkin spice latte in me RIGHT NOW." Her loud voice assaults my eardrum through the phone, and I quietly turn down the volume.

As one of the three hair stylists in town, she knows just about anything and everything there is to know about the shallow people of Hallow Grove. Two months ago, when Tom, the fire chief, cheated on his wife, Sloan was the first to know. His mistress was her client at the time, and Sloan watched the young woman's phone over her shoulder while Tom texted her some seriously raunchy messages. Of course, Sloan called me immediately after and spilled the beans, repeating their messages word for word like she had a photographic memory. It was one of our favorite small-town secrets up until his wife caught him, and the whole town found out in a matter of hours.

Piping hot tea travels fast in a town as compact and tightly knit as Hallow Grove.

"They better not be out of pumpkin syrup this time!" I whine into the phone as I dip my hand back inside the jack-o'-lantern. I fumble around with the lighter as I try to spark it, grunting under my breath while I struggle.

"Don't remind me," Sloan groans through clenched teeth. "Praline lattes are good and all, but they don't measure up to pumpkin spice lattes on a nippy fall day. I won't settle for anything less on Devil's Night."

I shake my head, grinning at my best friend. "I know you won't. I'll finish lighting this pumpkin, then I'll leave. See you in ten minutes."

"Sounds good," she giggles before abruptly ending our phone call.

The line goes dead, and I turn my attention back toward getting this pumpkin lit. I press my thumb against the metal spark wheel, dragging it toward the ignition. It doesn't light, so I shake it around in my hand, then flick it again. The wheel rolls, and I hear the tiny flame ignite.

Peering through the side of the pumpkin where I've carved a mouth full of sharp teeth, I guide the small fire toward the candle wick. My fingernail begins to heat against the flame and I'm forced to hover at an awkward angle. The wick quickly turns black against the flame, and I impatiently wait as the seconds tick by, silently begging it to catch fire before I singe the tip of my thumb.

"Fuck!" I curse as the wick lights, and I yank my hand away, waving it through the air in an attempt to cool my hot flesh.

I hear a deep voice clear its throat behind me, and I turn to take a look, clutching my burnt hand to my chest.

My eyes fall upon my neighbor, Jim, lazily walking his dog, and I immediately notice the disgusted look on his wrinkled face as he watches me. His judgmental gaze drifts away from me and wanders across my yard, scanning my bold choices of Halloween décor. He frowns before returning his eyes to me, serving one last unapproving look.

My hip pops to the side, and I throw him an overly enthusiastic wave with my wounded hand as a fake bitch smile washes across my face. "Hey, neighbor," I yell across my lawn.

Jim's back straightens, and his eyes widen as I acknowledge his pathetic existence. Instead of returning my greeting like any good neighbor would do, he turns on his heel and begins yanking on the leash attached to his equally lazy English bulldog, Gary.

I'm typically a dog person, but Gary doesn't do it for me.

No tricks, no treats, no salutations. Nothing.

I've tried to make friends with him through treats and ear scratches, but he's an exact replica of Jim. I'm fairly certain all they do is walk around the block once or twice a day, then return home to pig out on junk food and sleep. On the days I've been grossly unlucky and found myself downwind of him, I would've been willing to bet Jim doesn't shower either.

My smile rapidly fades as Jim and Gary turn the corner, frantically trying to remove themselves from my sight. Glancing back down at my jack-o'-lantern, I realize it lit when I burnt the fuck out of my hand.

"Thank God," I whisper as I stride toward my front door. All I need is my black leather jacket, my wallet, and the keys to my Elantra; then, I'll be on my way to meet Sloan.

The warmth of my central heating system blasts against my face as I step inside, and I feel instant relief from the icy wind. I should've worn my jacket outside to light the pumpkins, but I was too excited to get out there. They're my most prized possessions right now, and I had to make sure they were glowing and perfect before meeting Sloan for pumpkin spice lattes.

My wallet and keys are resting beside my jacket on the back of my mouse grey L-shaped couch. I slip my arms through the jacket sleeves, wiggling as I tug it over my shoulders. Snatching my belongings off the couch, I listen to my boots clack against the wood floors as I make my way back to the front door.

The unwelcoming breeze hits my face as I step outside, but it doesn't seem to bother me as much now that I've got a jacket on. Some years we've got snow by now, so I'm grateful the mild weather is holding on a bit longer. Sloan and I have parties to attend this weekend.

Lucy, my Elantra, is parked in the driveway that extends outward from the garage which I've turned into my own personal storage unit. I click the "unlock" button on the key fob, and the lights flash as my little black car obeys. Slipping into the driver's seat, I throw my wallet in the center console before inserting my key into the ignition.

As I turn it, Lucy comes to life, roaring her small but fierce 2.0-liter engine. My Halloween playlist immediately begins to play as my phone connects to Bluetooth, and I crank the volume while backing out of my driveway.

The drive from my house to Rustic Roast is less than five minutes with light traffic, and it's an enjoyable little journey. I pass through a neighborhood of cottage-style family homes before entering downtown Hallow Grove, where the heart of the town resides. Most of our town events are held in the square, and if they're big enough, the mayor shuts down the main streets for people to wander down aimlessly while celebrating whatever small-town festivity he decided was worthy enough of closing down the town.

There's a white Tahoe trying to back out of a parking spot just down the road from the coffee shop, so I slam on my brakes before I pass them, allowing them to gift me their prime parking spot. They're slow to remove themselves from my newly claimed space, but eventually they speed off, and I whip in.

Sloan is tapping away on her phone just outside the entrance, blissfully unaware I've arrived.

"BOO!" I shout as I throw my hands toward her, reaching out like I'm about to snatch her soul.

She jumps into the air, screeching as her phone flies out of her hands. She fumbles for it, but I've already caught it mid-air before it can hit the ground, all the while laughing hysterically at how easily she frightens.

She shoves my shoulder as she snatches her phone from my hands. "You scared the shit out of me, you spooky bitch!"

Shrugging, I chuckle, "It's Devil's Night! Would you expect anything less from me?"

"True," she nods, pursing her lips as she squints her eyes at me. "Let's get our pumpkin spice fix." Sloan twists toward the front entrance and jams her phone into her designer purse, swinging the door open as she struts through. A bell chimes above our heads, alerting the staff they've got new customers, but we're regulars here, and they already know what we've come for.

I roll my eyes, still laughing, as I follow her through the glass door. We don't waste any time as we cross the coffee shop floor, heading straight for the "order here" sign. Sloan is already ordering our drinks by the time I wipe the overly amused grin off my face.

"Can I get two large pumpkin spice lattes?" she asks Juan, a barista we've come to know well, behind the register. "Hot!" she adds before he can ask how we'd like our drinks.

I notice what looks like a mischievous smirk cross his face. He glances between us, and then he nods before turning around to grab two large coffee cups hidden on the counter behind him.

"I just finished making them. I knew you ladies would be here soon, and we're starting to run low on pumpkin syrup. After the last time we ran out, I figured you two would kill me if I didn't have your drinks piping hot and ready when you got here." He passes each of us a warm coffee cup with our names written down the sides. "They're on the house tonight."

My eyes light up as I flash Juan an impressed smile. "That's very sweet, Juan. Thank you."

"This makes up for last time," Sloan announces between eye-fluttering sips of scalding hot latte. "But you're not off the hook if it happens again, for future reference."

He chuckles, amused with Sloan's overly direct personality. "I'll have to keep a secret stash in the back just for you," he winks, catering to Sloan's drama.

A sly smirk forms on her lips as she nods with approval. "That's more like it."

Together, we turn to walk down the tight aisle wedged between wooden chairs. I follow behind Sloan as she nudges chairs out of our way, carefully slipping past a few happy customers. I'm mostly watching my feet as I shuffle down the aisle, being sure not to catch myself on a stray leg.

"Does this work?" Sloan asks as she stops just ahead of me.

I glance up from the floor for the first time, and instead of searching for the table in question, my eyes pause as they pass over a paralyzingly handsome stranger.

He's already watching me through whiskey-brown eyes, scanning over every inch of my body like I'm some prized possession he's contemplating purchasing. Warmth rises to my cheeks as his sharp facial features and intricately tattooed skin lure me in. I can't help but suck my lip between my teeth. He's the most pleasantly appealing person I've seen in this small town for a long time, although I suppose that's not saying too much considering the pathetic pool of men there is to pick from here in Hallow Grove, but the point is, he's hot as fuck.

My knees begin to wobble, weakening as I clench my thighs together mid-step, seeking relief from the pressure building between them. He chooses that moment to make eye contact with me, and a devilishly charming smirk spreads across his full, filled out lips. One split-second glance, and it's like he already knows how devastatingly enthralled I am with him. My breath catches in the back of my throat as he flashes wickedly white teeth at me. Releasing my bottom lip from between my teeth, I return the gesture with the most flirtatious smile I can manage while being completely consumed by this stranger.

We're both stuck in a trance for a brief moment as I pass. It's like I'm moving in slow motion, and the seconds seem to last far longer than they should. He's covered in tattoos, but my attention is drawn toward a small cross under his right eye, and the line work on it is so clean I know he didn't get it from anyone around here. I'm the only one with line work that clean, and I sure as hell would remember tattooing the face of a man this gorgeous.

Sloan's voice pulls me back into reality. "Does this work?" she repeats, louder this time, as she scrapes a wooden chair across the floor.

I swallow hard, reluctantly breaking locked eyes with the man. I find Sloan, and she's watching me with the most intrigued look on her face. Her head is cocked at a steep angle, and there's a wickedly entertained curve to her lips.

"Yes," I choke out, trying my best to shake off the intensity of the look I just exchanged with a stranger, a stranger who will now be sitting behind me. It takes me a

13

moment to regroup, but I finally get there. "There's no better place to people-watch than by the window," I force out.

She's still staring at me with amusement twinkling in her eyes. She glances between me and the strange man now seated behind me, discretely letting me know she witnessed our moment.

"So listen," she starts as she diverts her attention back to me. "I know you're nervous about tonight, but I really think it'll be good for you to get out. You can't hide out in that creepy, old house forever. It's bad for your health to spend so much time alone."

I roll my eyes as I take a long sip of my latte. She's being sarcastic, but not really. Sloan thinks my house is haunted and sucks the light out of me, but we both know that's just part of my personality some days. "I don't know how I feel about seeing Jonah at the party. I'd rather stay in and watch a horror movie."

Sloan doesn't know that I've been secretly fucking Jonah since last fall, and I'd like to keep my secret long enough to get the guts to finally kick Jonah to the curb. There aren't feelings involved, but for whatever the reason, I can't force myself to get rid of him. Every time I convince myself I don't need a fuck buddy, he's calling me up late at night when I'm already lying in bed with my vibrator, desperate for male touch. Alcohol and Jonah, while Sloan or anyone else is there to lay witness, is not a good combination, and if I'm smart, I'll keep myself in line.

She shakes her head at me, furrowing her brows. "You're coming with me. We already have the perfect costumes picked out, and I can't show up alone knowing Alex will be there."

Alex: Sloan's current fixation. He's tall, dirty blonde, and has good style, according to Sloan. He's also filthy rich, and I swear, sometimes all she sees are dollar signs when she looks at men.

I want to argue, but I can't be the bitch that forces her bestie to go to a party alone knowing damn well her crush is going to be there. I'm a better friend than that, even if it means I have to actively avoid Jonah all night.

"Fine," I sigh, throwing my hands up in defeat. "But, you're driving. I hate driving to the Miller house at night. The gravel roads are too narrow going around the lake."

"Deal," she beams before taking another swig of her latte. Her brow raises as she looks up from her cup. She assesses me up and down for a few seconds before saying,

"You need to get laid tonight. It's been too long, and your vibrator is going to give out soon if you don't give it a break."

Instinctively, I grab her wrist, crouching forward as I shush her. Damn Sloan and her loud-ass voice for always embarrassing me at the most inconvenient times. Of course, she'd want to talk about my trusty vibrator while the hottest guy I've ever seen is sitting behind me, without a doubt well within earshot.

"We will see what happens, but I make no promises. It depends on who shows up and how much alcohol I need to ingest before any of them become tolerable enough to fuck."

She lets out a loud bout of laughter, holding her hand over her chest as she tries to reel in her breathing. "That might be the most relatable thing you've ever said," she praises as she wipes a joyful tear from her waterline. "This is why we're best friends. I love your fucked up sense of humor."

"I know," I smile through bright eyes as I shrug my shoulders, cupping my warm pumpkin spice latte in my hands. Bringing the lid to my parted lips, I draw out a sweet, pumpkiny mouthful, swishing it around my mouth before swallowing. I lock eyes with the tattooed god sitting at the back of the café as I slowly lick the cream that had made its way down my lip, off my finger. Somehow I just know he'd put my vibrator to shame.

Staying away from Jonah is my top priority tonight.

Chapter Two
RHETT

After two painful hours of trying to hack into an overseas bank account the local Don Leon Cartel has been using, I'm still no closer. This cafe's shitty Wi-Fi connection makes it damn near impossible to run the programs I need to crack the codes and follow the wire transfers. Add in the fact that my head is pounding and every time the small bell on the door chimes, signaling someone is coming or going, or the hissing sound of steam meets my ears, the gnawing feeling in my brain only gets worse.

Leaning back in the wooden chair, I watch the traffic drive by the large window beside my table. My midnight black 750 GSXR sport bike is parked across the street in front of my apartment, and it stands out like a sore thumb in this dull town, but I never go anywhere without it. That's my baby.

Grabbing the small ceramic mug from the table, I inhale the aromatic scent of premium dark roast before bringing it to my lips. I swirl the steaming black coffee around my tongue, savoring its roasted taste before swallowing it. This shit is better than a bottle of aspirin, which is unexpected in a little farm town like this one.

I wasn't happy about being sent here. Small towns aren't my scene, and Hallow Grove is as small as they come. There's nothing here for me, just endless fields of corn and air that stinks of animal shit, but after a few days here, I can see why the Don Leon Cartel has made this their new headquarters. No one would think to look in some tiny town in the middle of nowhere while searching for them.

No one except me, that is.

There is no place on Earth these fuckers could go where I wouldn't follow. My sole mission in life has been to destroy the entire operation and kill their incompetent leader. After all, a life for a life is fair, and he took my father's life, so now a debt is owed to me. The only saving grace I've had for the last week is this goddamn café and its black coffee, but that's partially bittered by just how bad the

Wi-Fi is here. It might as well be dial-up with how hard it is to stay connected long enough to actually get anything done.

I down the last of my coffee and place the empty mug on the table before running my inked hand through my hair, pushing it back from my face as I glance around the café. It's pretty busy this evening; there are more people out and about than usual. Some are dressed in costumes, others in regular attire, all wanting their caffeine fix before tonight's festivities—Devil's Night.

Back home, this night would be spent with teens trashing people's yards, tossing eggs at houses and hurtling toilet paper over trees. It's a pastime I may have indulged in once or twice in my youth, but I don't expect that to happen here, not in such a small, tight-knit town.

With my coffee gone and the Wi-Fi as useless as it could possibly be, I begin packing my belongings back into my duffle bag so that I can return to my apartment across the street.

The bell on the door signals another customer has entered the café, and at first, I pay no mind to it, continuing to sort my things away, but when a soft laugh meets my ears, the world seems to freeze for everyone but me.

Lifting my eyes from my laptop, I'm met with the most beautiful woman I've ever seen. Long, dark hair flows behind her as she trails behind her redhead friend to the counter. I watch as they order their drinks, and the moment she smiles at the barista as he hands her coffee over the counter… something deep inside me stirs.

All it takes is one look, a split second where another man holds her attention, to send me into a downward spiral of jealousy and rage. I never want her to smile at anyone else like that again, unless it's me.

Oversized coffee cups in hand, they make their way down the narrow aisle beside me, passing tables full of people. As she passes, I catch a glimpse of the paper cup she's holding. Her name is scribbled on the side in a black marker: Cara.

A beautiful name for a beautiful girl. I can't help but run my eyes across her perfect, supple body, from her black boots to her perky tits she keeps hidden behind a tight leather jacket.

"Does this work?" The redhead asks, getting no response from my new fixation. I'm met with her ghostly grey eyes as I reach her face, and her piercing gaze sends a chill down my spine.

Fuck, she caught me.

Women in these small towns are different, more reserved, and uptight. They usually call me a perve or tell me to fuck off when they catch me eye fucking them, but not her.

No, she's different.

She's special, she sees me.

Accepts me.

Instead of telling me off, she catches me off guard, keeping her eyes locked with mine, challenging me as she pulls her plump bottom lip into her mouth, sucking it between her pearly teeth. I flash her a coy smirk that she promptly returns with a flirty little smile.

Fuck. This girl wants me.

The metal barb of my Jacob's Ladder piercing rubs against the confinement of my tight black skinny jeans as my cock hardens at the subtle, but incredibly sexy gesture.

She wants to play.

It takes everything in me not to turn in my chair and watch her as she leaves my sight.

"Does this work?" The redhead repeats again with a louder tone this time.

"Yes," my girl quickly answers, trying to seem like she isn't completely consumed by me.

My heart races at the sound of the wooden chair legs scraping against the floor beneath the table directly behind me, signaling where they plan to sit. Lowering my eyes to the floor, a coy smirk forms on my face knowing full well her silence is a direct response to our little moment. I can't blame her for being so speechless after locking eyes with me. I know I'm good-looking and taller than most men, a feature I can thank my late father for; add in that all of my free time is spent in the gym, where I work hard to maintain my well-toned body, and it doesn't take much for women to swoon over me.

I've always said there are two types of women in this world: The ones that take a single look at a guy like me and run, and those who fantasize about having me buried deep between their thighs.

As for ones who fall at my feet with just one look, I'm usually more than happy to give them whatever they want, to bring any fantasy to life, especially when it saves me from having to scroll through pages upon pages on Pornhub before finally finding something I can actually stroke my dick to.

I've stuck my dick in more women than I can count, but that's all it's ever been. Fuck, chuck, and onto the next. Not with this girl, though. She's something else, something new and interesting, and from the moment I saw her, the moment our eyes locked and she bit down on that goddamn plump lip, I knew that one fuck would never be enough.

It's clear she sees me for me and accepts who I am. No one has done that since my father died. No one has looked at me in the same way she did and seen me as a person, until her. This need to own her has taken root in the deepest parts of me, instantly sealing her fate to mine.

Even with my devilishly handsome good looks, this pretty little thing is still too perfect for me. If I want to keep her, she needs to be marked and broken, and when she locked eyes with me, I knew she wanted it to be me who ultimately ruins her. In those few seconds, her ghostly eyes told me all the things her mouth couldn't, and I'll spend the rest of my days watching her, touching her pristine inked skin, and claiming her, whether she allows me to or not.

She's mine.

They continue their conversation as they sit down, and I adjust myself in the wooden chair. Opening my laptop, I pull a binder and pen back out from my duffle bag, trying my best to blend in and not seem suspicious as I listen in on their exchange of words.

"So listen, I know you're nervous about tonight, but I really think it'll be good for you to get out. You can't hide out in that creepy, old house forever. It's bad for your health to spend so much time alone," her friend explains with a tone filled with concern and with a hint of desperation.

"I don't know how I feel about seeing Jonah at the party. I'd rather stay in and watch a horror movie," my girl responds. My blood instantly boils at the sound of another man's name slipping from her lips.

Who is Jonah, and why does my girl want to avoid him?

"You're coming with me. We already have the perfect costumes picked out, and I can't show up alone knowing Alex will be there," her persistent friend pushes.

The pressure she's placing on my girl leaves a bad taste in my mouth, but the thought of seeing my girl dressed up for me, well, that sends all the right signals straight to my dick.

"Fine, but you're driving. I hate driving to the Miller house at night. The gravel roads are too narrow going around the lake," she gives in with a sigh, and it's clear she isn't excited about this party.

I slide my iPhone from my pocket and quickly type in the four-digit pin to unlock it. Opening my browser, I bring up satellite maps of Hallow Grove, Iowa, and begin my search for lakes in the area. Finding only two, I close in on the first one, small and secluded, with no buildings in the area or any marked roads.

Not the one I'm looking for.

I zoom out and slide my finger across the screen until I reach the other lake. Zooming back in, I find what appears to be a narrow, one-car-wide gravel road wrapping around the north side of the lake leading to a massive, secluded property.

Opening another browser window, I bring up the county assessor website, typing in several codes to get me past their weak firewalls and into the content not accessible to just anyone. Being a white hat hacker for the CIA has its benefits. Even if my hacking gets flagged, they won't be able to do anything about it. When it comes to breaking into websites or files, I'm basically untouchable.

Sure enough, the deed on the county website shows the house belongs to a Brandon Miller.

Bingo.

I close the tab and reopen the satellite map, marking the lake house with a pin, and then I save it directly to my iPhone.

"Deal," her friend says excitedly. "You need to get laid tonight. It's been too long, and your vibrator is going to give out soon if you don't give it a break."

I smile, saving the directions to the party to my phone as the sounds of my girl trying to shush her friend hit my ears.

Don't worry, little nightmare, you won't need that vibrator. Not after tonight.

Lucky for her, the café is loud, and I doubt anyone else heard her friend's little remark, although I'm happy I did.

"We'll see what happens, but I make no promises. It depends on who shows up and how much alcohol I need to ingest before any of them become tolerable enough to fuck," my girl says loudly, almost like she wanted me to hear.

It's an invitation to show up. It's her way of telling me she wants me there. Little does she know I was showing up regardless of her invite.

I know what she needs, what she wants.

Her friend's laugh rings out across the coffee shop, "That might be the most relatable thing you've ever said. This is why we're best friends. I love your fucked up sense of humor."

"I know," my girl laughs.

Her laughter is alluring and soft, almost ethereal, like sparks from a roaring fire floating up to the night sky. My skin burns for her, and even though I know nothing about her, I have to have her. She wants me too; I can see it in her eyes and hear it in the tone of her voice.

I will have her.

I sit up straight in my chair, confident in the bit of information I've gained from their short conversation. My body is pumping with adrenaline and anticipation for tonight. I've always loved surveillance and the thrill of seeing people when they think they're unseen. The shit people do when they think no one is watching is fucking surprising, but this already feels different than the people I watch on a daily basis. She feels different. Something about her has me fully enthralled. One look and I'm completely obsessed.

They talk for a bit more, and I listen in here and there, easily picking up any relevant information regarding my new obsession. I find out she's a tattoo artist, the best in Hallow Grove, too, by the sound of it. I've also come to learn that her friend loves to gossip, and being a hairstylist apparently means she gets the lowdown at work of all the shady happenings in this shit hole. Thankfully my girl doesn't seem to care much for the drama, but gives her friend her best attempt at a genuinely shocked reaction to the town's latest scandals.

After a while, the scraping of chairs moving against the floor meets my ears again, letting me know they've risen from the table behind me. Her friend walks past me first, her long red hair flowing down her back as she struts down the aisle carrying an empty cup. She places it in the trash bin beside the register before chatting up the same barista as before, making sure to push her large tits together between her arms as she leans over the counter.

I know her type, the tryhards with low self-esteem, who flaunt what they have to get what they want, and if you refuse, they try harder.

Shuffling behind me pulls my attention as my girl leaves the table and walks down the aisle next to me without glancing back. I don't take it to heart. I know she's trying to ignore the fact that we had a moment. She's playing hard to get, but we both know what she wants. I watch her perfectly tight little ass sway with her hips as she walks, leaving a scented trail of cinnamon and vanilla behind her, silently calling my name as she joins her friend at the counter.

As she reaches her redhead friend, she slowly turns to face me, bringing her cup to her lips and taking a sip as pumpkin sweet cream drips down her lips. She raises her eyes to mine, keeping them fixated on me as she wipes the cream from her lip with her finger, and sucks it off. My cock twitches at the sight of her with cream dripping down her luscious lips. I sit forward, entranced by this risky game my girl is playing in a place as public as this.

It should be my cream dripping down her.

She wants it to be my cream.

My jaw clicks with excitement. A genuine smile forms on my face as I shake my head at her. She returns my smile, and I nod slightly in her direction, ensuring she knows I see her, too. Her face flushes a gorgeous shade of pink, and she quickly turns her eyes away, grabbing hold of her friend's arm. My girl is embarrassed easily.

Oh, this is going to be fun.

I watch, keeping my eyes fixated on her as she patiently waits for her friend to finish harassing the barista before they open the café door, setting off the familiar bell sound and heading outside.

I waste no time shoving my things back into the duffle bag, eager to get the night started, to find out who this Jonah fucker is, and to see my girl again, only this time all dressed up and ready for me to ruin.

With my things all packed away safely secured in my duffle bag, I lift my now numb ass from the wooden chair as my large frame pushes the chair backward. I stretch my arms out above my head; the action has the front of my shirt lifting a bit, giving the older women at the table next to me a nice view of the v-cut above my jeans. They gasp with disgust, shaking their heads at me with disapproval but deep down, we all know they secretly love the little show they're getting. They'll be running home to their husbands, all hot and bothered for the first time in probably months. I give them a good smirk, making a point to show them I'm happy to help give their practically dead libidos a much-needed kick-start before grabbing my bag and tossing it over my shoulder.

They quickly turn away, shielding their eyes as they act repulsed, pretending that looking at me might bring them shame in such a small town, which makes me smile more. People care too much for what others think of them, and it's amusing to me how they can spend their lives shoving down parts of themselves, keeping them hidden to please others.

Growing up, I was picked on and bullied. Kids always thought my obsession with watching people and my love for tech and computers was weird and made me a nerd, but my father taught me not to care, and to not let the thoughts of others dictate how I choose to live my life.

"A lion does not lose sleep over the thoughts of sheep," is what he used to tell me, a quote he'd learned earlier in his life, and he was right; since that day, I've not lost sleep over anyone.

Until now.

I can already see the signs of how my new obsession, Cara, will be impossible to shake from my thoughts. It's unusual how intrigued I am with a girl who hides behind the sweet small-town girl façade and what truly lies in the depths behind it. To some, she may be the girl of their dreams, the perfect girl next door, but to me, she is the monster under my bed, the thing that keeps me up at night.

My little nightmare.

I cross the room to the front of the counter, handing my empty mug to the barista who exchanged smiles with my girl earlier.

"Thanks so much for visiting Rustic Roast. Hope we see you again," he says with an overly cheerful smile.

I return his thanks with a stern look while I picture how good it would feel to filet the smile from his face. As if sensing my tension, he turns pale and heads back to his register, where he continues to take orders from the never-ending line of people.

Returning my thoughts to my mission, I head to the door, push it open, and quickly head out into the cool fall night. I pull my cigarettes from the pocket of my leather jacket, placing one between my lips, and tuck the small pack back in my pocket. Reaching my other hand into the opposite pocket, I pull out a sterling silver zippo lighter, the only thing I have left of my father, and flick the lid back before striking it, lighting my cig. I inhale, letting my eyes fall closed as my lungs fill with tobacco and nicotine, calming myself.

When I open them, I scan the still busy streets until I see a small cart outside a clothing store across the street. The cart is full of Halloween costumes, and it just so happens that I'm in need of one if I want to meet my girl at this party. Looking both ways, I quickly jog across the street, reaching the cart and the older woman running it.

"Everything is half off, dear," she explains as I browse the masks.

Clowns, ghost faces, weird ones with huge noses, all overused and don't give off the impression I want to make. I scour the racks of masks over and over until, finally, I find the right one. A scarecrow, perfect for a town like this, and just the right amount of eerie I need.

I toss the woman a fifty, telling her to keep the change, and quickly make my way back up the street to my apartment to ready myself for tonight.

I am a predator unwilling to share his prey, and by the sounds of their conversation tonight, someone else thinks they have a claim to what's mine. Tonight, I change that and make sure she knows who she belongs to.

My little nightmare is mine, and only mine.

Chapter Three
CARA

"It's over here!" Sloan shouts from across my bedroom. She plucks one of my monster erotica novels off my nightstand, allowing the pages to spread, revealing my lighter as they slip open. "You hid it inside one of your monster smut books," she laughs, snatching it from between the pages, then waves it through the air.

I keep a few lighters stashed in my room to create the moody fall ambiance I so desperately crave during the spooky season, but I've used them so frequently that they've all run dry of lighter fluid. The exception is this one, which, apparently, I thought would make a good bookmark as I was falling asleep last night.

"There's a double peen in that book," I admit with a mischievous grin. "You can borrow it when I'm done."

Cocking my head to the side, I shrug, winking as a horrified look crosses Sloan's face.

She fakes a gag. "I think I'll pass."

She's not into dark romance or monster smut like I am, but I continue to taunt her with the filthy details written within the pages of my favorite books. Half of the time, she turns pale at the gory, unnerving details, and the other half, she simply rolls her eyes, silently praying I'm not as fucked up in the head as I sound.

I am, but I prefer to keep that to myself.

"Do you still have the red lipstick I wore to the Christmas party last year?" Sloan asks as she sits on the ground facing my full length mirror with a big black bag jammed full of makeup. She begins rustling around inside the bag, pulling out her favorite cosmetics one at a time. "I think that shade of red will match my top."

I nod, crossing the room toward my bathroom to retrieve it for her. "I was thinking about wearing a shimmery pink gloss. It would match my 'angel' aesthetic," I say as I gesture toward my slutty Halloween costume.

I'm dressed in a scandalous white top that covers the same amount of skin a bra would, but according to the description on the packaging, it's an "angelic crop top."

Lies.

It's a cheaply made silky white bra equipped with double padding to make my tits look extra perky. A small set of silver feather wings are attached to my back, doing little to cover the excessive amount of skin I'm showing. My mini skirt matches the bra perfectly, covering my ass just enough to give horny party-goers a little show. Underneath my skirt, I've pulled on opaque thigh-high tights complete with diamond rhinestones. My tattoos are still visible through the sheer tights, and I like the way the diamonds shine against my own artwork. Tattooing myself is never easy, but I enjoy the challenge it creates, and at the end of the day, there's no one within a hundred mile radius I would trust more than myself to inject permanent ink into my skin.

Sloan's devil costume counters me immaculately. She has the same bra and skirt, but the fabric has been dyed a blood-red color, while her wings are an even deeper shade of red.

"Here," I say, extending my arm toward Sloan as I hold the red lipstick out for her to take.

She turns and takes it quickly, tossing it into the pile of cosmetics she formed beside her crossed legs. I cringe slightly when I hear the tube clack against the hard mound of plastic. Sloan owns what I estimate to be thousands of dollars worth of makeup, and I own a few statement pieces, but tend to stick to the cheaper stuff. While my collection is small, I'm a lot kinder to mine than Sloan is. She tosses her high-dollar cosmetics around as though they're easily replaced, and sometimes she forgets that what's mine isn't necessarily what's hers.

I plop myself down onto my black comforter, leaning back on my hands as I patiently wait for Sloan to get ready. Watching her apply a full mask of makeup is like watching an experienced artist create a new masterpiece on a blank canvas. I joke about her shapeshifting abilities, but it's not really all that far off when I take into account all the contour sticks and highlighter she uses. We sit in silence for a few minutes while I watch the master at work, blending various shades of grey against her eyelids after carving out her favorite facial features.

Breaking our silence when she's almost done, I gently laugh, reminiscing on our childhood. "Do you remember that one Halloween when we dressed up as witches and glued warts to our faces? We thought we were so badass."

Sloan bursts out into a loud belly laugh, spraying a line of spit directly onto my mirror. "Yeah, and we wore those horrendous lime green tights under oversized black muumuus. Who let us out of the house like that?"

Throwing my head back, I can't help but smile as I picture our pre-pubescent era. Sloan and I have been through it all together. Losing our virginities, bad breakups, braces… everything. She's my ride-or-die. "I'm pretty sure your mom has a picture of it in one of her photo albums."

"She has a picture of every dumb thing we've ever done." There's an amused twinkle in Sloan's eyes; I can see through her reflection in the mirror. "She'd die if she saw what we're wearing right now."

Sloan's mother is one of the most religiously devout Christians of Hallow Grove, spending the majority of her time on her knees praying to a god I'm not sure I follow, but I can't openly admit that. Not here, at least. I wouldn't put it past this little town to try to stone me to death for questioning the idea of God. "She's probably too busy cleansing her house of demons."

"Mmm, p-probably," Sloan pops the "p" as she applies my lipstick over her thin lips, taking extra time to crispen the over-lined edges. Changing the subject, she asks, "Do you think we should bring jackets?"

Shaking my head, I say, "And cover up these gloriously slutty costumes? I don't think so. It's not supposed to be that cold, and there's always a big bonfire anyway. We could always stay near it if we need to." As a final thought, I add, "We just need to make sure we don't get so drunk we fall in."

Sloan uses her hands to shove herself off the ground, leaving the pile of cosmetics at her feet as she rises. "Devils like to play with fire," she jokes, pointing toward her costume.

There's a smidge of sternness in my voice as I respond, "Drunk Sloan needs to forget about that. You always do stupid shit when you're drunk, and I really don't want to pull your burnt corpse out of a bonfire tonight while half the people we went to high school with watch."

"You're probably right," she admits, lowering her eyes to the ground as she goes deep in thought. "But, you do some stupid shit when you're drunk, too, you know. Last year it was you who jumped into the lake wearing nothing but an oversized white t-shirt and a lime-green thong."

I open my bedroom door, allowing her to stroll through the doorway ahead of me in the usual overly dramatic Sloan fashion. "If we're not careful, I'll do it again," I chuckle under my breath, following her out the door.

We walk through the house laughing and teasing each other about the poor judgment calls our drunk personas continuously make. Passing by the kitchen on our way out, I decide I need a bit of liquid courage. I veer to the right, turning into the large open space.

"I need a shot," I announce as Sloan doubles back, entering the kitchen behind me.

"We need a shot," she promptly corrects me while she begins searching through my liquor stash.

Pulling two small glasses from my cabinet, I place them on the counter in front of me and patiently wait for Sloan to join me with her selection of alcohol.

She turns away from the liquor cart abruptly, holding up a half-empty bottle of tequila.

"No," I say, shaking my head in disgust while raising my hands. "I can't do tequila. You know I can't do tequila."

Unscrewing the lid at record speed, she flicks it off the top of the bottle with her acrylic fingernail. It hits the

41

black granite counter, spinning in place for a moment before coming to a stop.

"You can," Sloan raises her eyebrow at me as she begins pouring the clear liquid into our shot glasses. "And you will," she says as she slides the full glass toward me.

I grasp the glass between my fingers, lifting it to my nose. The pungent scent stings my nostrils, forcing my entire face to scrunch.

Sloan raises the glass to her lips, stopping to make brief eye contact with me before throwing both her head and the shot back, swallowing it all in one gulp. She doesn't even cringe, giving me false hope for what's about to slide down my throat.

I can't pussy out. I'm the hardcore, tattooed friend, and she's the bougie queen. It would damage my bad-bitch ego to let her show me up with a tequila shot. Slowly bringing the glass to my painted lips, I squeeze my eyes shut as I catapult the liquid to the back of my throat as quickly as I can. It stings as it slides off my tongue, rolling down the back of my throat in sloshy waves. It feels like I've swallowed a blender blade, and now it's ripping through the flesh, coating my throat. Sloan beams at me from across the counter, visibly proud of me for taking her challenge.

"Ahh," I cringe as I internally crumple into the tiniest wad of paper. "Next time, I'll pick the liquor."

"That's fair," she laughs as we leave the kitchen, heading toward my newly painted black front door.

As soon as Sloan opens the door, there's a blast of cold air that fills the house, running between the holes in our mesh tights. Goosebumps rise along nearly every inch of my skin while the hair on the back of my neck seems to rise. Rattling chills slither down my spine, and I catch myself reaching for my coat next to the door.

Sloan's hand comes down on mine, slapping me away from the warm fabric. "You're the one that said no jackets," she reminds me, turning back toward the direction of her car parked outside. "And it's not that cold."

Rolling my eyes, I scoff as I step through the doorway and into the chilly breeze. I'm sure to lock the door behind me, gripping and twisting it to double-check it's secure. There's a tingle that remains on the back of my neck, and I feel a faint sense of danger.

Chapter Four
RHETT

The microwave beep echoes loudly throughout my nearly empty apartment, signaling that my poor excuse of a dinner is ready. I turn the knob on the bathroom door, then walk through the open living room and into the kitchen.

My apartment is tiny, nothing fancy, just a small bachelor apartment above a quaint little shop, but it's all I need. It's basically one large room, save for the miniscule bathroom toward the back of the room. The studio space is a living room and bedroom combo, and the open concept kitchen is complete with a breakfast bar. It's bare and clean, just the way I like it. I never stay in one place long enough to bother with pictures or personal belongings. I have my equipment, my blades, my bike, and my clothes. I don't need anything else.

Reaching the microwave, I swing the door open just as it's about to beep again, sparing my eardrums from the most annoying noise ever. I grab the plate of steaming leftover Chinese food before closing the door with my other hand, then grabbing the fork I left on the counter. I cross the kitchen to the breakfast bar, where my laptop is set up and plastered with pictures of my new obsession.

Since leaving the café a few hours ago, I've managed to hack into all her social media accounts and have gone through way too many conversations with friends and clients, but no family, from what I can tell. Sloan, the one I saw her with at the café, appears to be her childhood best friend and Jonah, that fucker, is her ex-boyfriend, who according to their recent dirty little conversations, is still fucking around with her.

I'll be changing that tonight.

I hungrily shovel down the food while clicking through pages upon pages of selfies and tagged posts, learning everything I can about my girl before I surprise her at the Devil's Night party later this evening. Based on her photos alone, it's clear she's Halloween-obsessed and a talented tattoo artist.

I might even have to convince her to add some ink to my collection… maybe her name across my cock.

When it comes to chatting with her clients, she's professional and polite, like a nice little girl. Knowing I'm going to ruin her has my cock itching to leave this minute, desperate to have her looking at me again the same way she did at the café. Picking up my dishes, I head to the sink to wash them quickly, knowing that if I don't do it now, it will only piss me off later knowing that I left them when I should have done them when I was done eating. Messes are one of my biggest pet peeves, and I cannot risk anything ruining my night tonight.

With the dishes and kitchen thoroughly cleaned, I make my way to the tiny bathroom and start up a hot shower. I strip down and step inside, letting the steaming water sting my skin as it cascades down my body. The bite from the scalding water on my skin mixed with thoughts of my little nightmare has my dick hard in no time. I grab the bar of soap from the shelf and lather my hands up with thick suds before running my hands across my body, starting with my arms and chest. I work my way down until I reach my rock-hard length. Slowly stroking from the base to the tip has me growling as my soapy hand slides over each piercing of my Jacob's Ladder.

There are six in total, and each one is more sensitive than the last as they get closer to the tip. I pump myself nice and slow, working myself up for a release I won't allow myself to have.

No.

My next release will be with my little nightmare, ruined and crying on my cock, begging me to stop while I fill her with my cum.

Once I'm freshly showered and dressed in my attire for the night: black jeans, a black tee, and my favorite leather jacket, I grab the scarecrow mask I bought earlier along with my favorite blade, Mori, and tuck them into the pocket of my jacket. Skipping out the door, I am eager to get the night's festivities started.

* * *

The lake house was easier to find than I thought it would be based on satellite images, and my girl was right; those roads around the lake are fucking brutal at night, especially on a bike. You'd think with the kind of money this Brandon Miller dude has, he would've paid to have the roads paved by now, but I guess he'd rather spend it on fancy lights and top of the line stereo systems. It seems as though Mr. Miller is trying to compensate for something...

The music blasts all around me and the bass thumps through my body as I climb off my bike, casually removing my matte black helmet. Placing it on the seat of my bike, I scan the crowds of people with a predatory gaze, searching for tonight's prey.

Everyone is already bombed by the looks of it, dancing in random places all over the yard. Some girls, desperate for attention, have even resorted to climbing on top of the picnic tables to dance in their slutty costumes, but none of them are my girl. She must not be here yet.

I lean myself against my bike and pull out my mask from inside my jacket, sliding it over my head with ease. My eyes are covered by a thin black mesh, allowing me to see out, but no one to see in. I turn my attention back on the partying crowds. A few cars down is an F150 with its tailgate down and a young couple practically fucking in the back of the truck while their friends drunkenly dance around them.

I smirk and shake my head; tonight is going to be good. Tonight is going to be easy.

As if right on cue, a car slowly rolls by me, then parks and out climbs my girl. In the most fitting costume, like she planned it just for me. A goddamn fucking angel.

My dick pulses in my pants, and I force myself to bite down hard on my lip beneath my mask at the sight of her as she opens the car door and steps out wearing a tiny little white corset top with a short white skirt. Paired with silver wings, a fluffy halo, and, as if her perfect little body in that downright sinful costume wasn't going to be drawing enough male attention, she has tiny rhinestones scattered about her perfectly toned legs.

She wanted to stand out. She wanted to make it easy for me to find her in the crowds of people as if she didn't stand out already.

Her long dark hair is hanging down her back in perfect waves, and all I can think about is how badly I want to run my hands through it while she's bent over in front of me. My girl could make any outfit look good, but this one, showing just enough skin for me to get a peek at some of the ink she has painted on her pristine skin, will forever be my favorite. She wore it for me. A little taste of what she keeps hidden behind her leather jacket. A peek at what's about to be mine.

Fuck, she is too perfect.

Her friend from the café, Sloan, follows suit, climbing out of the car wearing an almost identical red top with a slit up the front that can barely contain her huge tits, with two devil horns on her head.

They're laughing and giggling. My girl has the brightest, widest smile as they make their way through the crowds toward the house with their arms locked, and I can't wait to ruin it.

I follow them up the path to the large lake house, keeping myself far enough behind that I won't risk drawing their attention. The music gets louder the closer we get to the house, and at one point, I watch as my girl stops, using her friend's arm to keep her balance as she slides her cute little feet out of the strappy silver heels she paired with her outfit.

They reach the large log deck of the ranch-style home, stopping by the door to grab a few drinks each from the cooler before joining in on the party. Inside, the celebration is in full swing, the music so loud I can barely hear my own thoughts as I follow them through each of the rooms, watching them greet the people they pass.

My little nightmare seems nervous, and my guess is it has something to do with her little arrangement with Jonah, which I suspect her best friend knows nothing about. I learned from their text conversations that Sloan isn't Jonah's biggest fan, and from some of the shit she said about what he's pulled with my girl, I'm not surprised. The guy sounds like a real piece of shit, so of course I had to do some of my own research on him, and while he may not be the worst looking guy in this shit town, he's the typical small town, old money mama's boy. He's not good enough for my girl. There's nothing special about him except for maybe Cara, and after tonight, he won't even have her.

My eyes trail her through the waves of people as I stay hidden amongst the shadows the trees provide.

She approaches the bonfire with Sloan, rubbing her hands together before holding them out towards the flames, seeking warmth from the night's chill. The fire's glow illuminates her gorgeous eyes and pink cheeks as she stares aimlessly into the flames. People start to huddle up near the fire, blocking my view of my girl, so I retreat to the shadows in search of a new spot to watch her.

Cara's best friend is suddenly distracted by a lanky man in the distance, eye fucking her as he walks toward the house. There's an exchange of words between Cara and Sloan, leading Sloan to semi-reluctantly bounce her way inside the house, following the man like a loyal dog.

After a few minutes of battling the cold alone, she leaves the fire. She disappears inside and I quickly catch up, following her along the main level of the house, watching her tight little ass bounce as she makes her way from room to room until she stops at the punch bowl.

I find a shadowed corner with a perfect view and lean myself against the wooden wall. She sets down an empty beer bottle before grabbing a plastic cup from the table, using the ladle to fill her cups to the brim with the red liquid. She tosses it back, repeating the action at least twice more without hesitation.

Fuck, my girl can drink.

Watching her brings a proud smile to my face, discreetly hidden behind my scarecrow mask, until someone brushes up against me, pulling my attention from my prey.

"Hey baby, why yurr over here all by yourself? Come dance with me," the drunk bitch slurs as she hangs off my arm. "I love yurr mask, so scurry!"

I shrug her off my arm, annoyed that the first female touch I've received tonight isn't from my girl.

My little nightmare.

I turn my attention back to the small punch table while the sloppy drunk girl stumbles away searching for someone else to bother, but when I lay eyes on my girl, she isn't alone.

Some dude in a pumpkin mask is with her, and he has his arm wrapped around her waist. He has her pulled into his chest as he whispers something into her ear.

Jonah.

My blood boils beneath my skin, my heart beating like a Ferrari engine in an F1 race. She smiles at whatever bullshit he's feeding to her before he backs up, taking her hand in his as he leads her away from the table and through a large crowd of people. He pulls her up a lengthy staircase at the front of the house, and I follow closely behind them, keeping myself hidden and avoiding the flashing disco lights as I make my way up the staircase.

Reaching the top, they turn right, and for a brief moment, she's out of my sight, but not for long. I take the stairs two at a time, the party's music growing more faint the closer I get to the second floor. Finally, a break for my eardrums. I round the corner just in time to see them fade into a room at the end of the hall.

What the fuck?

I stalk down the hall like a man on a mission, and when I reach the wood door, I find they didn't even close it all the way.

Perfect.

Peeking through the crack, it appears to be a guest room with simple nightstands and a large bed against the only wall I can see through the tiny crack. They stop beside the bed, and my girl's perky little tits bounce as the bastard slams her back against the wall. My mouth waters at the sight of her- so goddamn delicious.

My eyes fixate on the swell of her breasts tucked tightly into the white corset top she wore for me tonight. My hands ache to touch them, to free them from the confinement of the white threads and take them into my mouth, roughly sinking my teeth into her plump flesh and marking her for everyone else to see.

My thoughts have my cock hardening until Jonah, because he wasn't annoying enough, brings himself in front of her, blocking my view like he was born to be a fucking cockblock.

But it's when his lips crash into hers that all the pleasant thoughts of my girl and her tits vanish, replaced by a burning need to burst through the door and take what's mine.

Chapter Five
CARA

The regret I feel for telling Sloan we didn't need jackets this evening is overpowering. It's somewhere around forty-five degrees, and I swear my nipples could cut diamonds. Sloan and I have been drinking by the bonfire since arriving well over an hour ago.

We showed up later than most, and by now, the strong majority of the party-goers are entering blackout mode. The pungent scent of alcohol swirls through the fall breeze, interlaced with the smoky aroma of the massive fire crackling beside the lake.

Looking around, this million-dollar lake house is a little blurry. The tequila shot Sloan pressured me into taking took the edge off my anxiety, and I've been suppressing it further by downing copious amounts of alcohol. Is this the best start to my decision-making this evening? Probably not, but I can't kick this eerie feeling that's been following me all day, and alcohol is helping, so that's what I'll go with for now.

There's an unusual chill tonight, and I don't think it's the autumn air. The only thing taming the hairs on the back of my neck is the continuous consumption of hard liquor.

The burn of cheap whiskey rolls down the back of my throat, clawing at my flesh as I swallow.

"Youuu need another drink," Sloan slurs as she grabs hold of my arm, stumbling around as she braces herself. "If you don't loosen up, you're going to make me lose my buzz, and I'm not ready for that."

I laugh, smiling at my unstable friend. "I think we're both more than 'buzzed' at this point. I'm not sure there's any going back from here. This is where the bad decision-making begins."

As if right on cue, Alex, Sloan's current infatuation, crosses the lawn, heading toward the house. He's eye fucking her as he walks, biting at his bottom lip as he sucks it between his teeth. He's tall and somewhat athletic, which blows the rest of these small-town losers out of the water. Most of the guys at this party grew up here and have never left, and nearly all of them still live with their mamas. They're not real men, and based on my experience, none of them know how to fuck.

Perhaps it's the alcohol, or maybe it's because Alex is genuinely good-looking, but I feel a smidge of jealousy as he watches my best friend. Alex isn't from here, and he's not like the rest of the "men" at this party. He's clean-cut and well put together, and Sloan says he's rich. What girl wouldn't want that kind of stability?

"Go hang out with him," I force out before my imagination gets the best of me. I shouldn't be jealous of my best friend.

"What?" Sloan snaps in a drunken state. "I can't just leave you here by yourself. Besties stick together at these things."

"Parties?" I laugh. "I'll be fine. You need to get laid, and I need to get another drink. I'll be out here when you're done with him."

She hesitantly draws her eyes away from him, making squinted eye contact with me. Her cheeks are flushed, an obvious effect of the alcohol raging its way through her bloodstream. "Are you sure?" she asks in the most sober voice she can pull together.

"Yes, I'm sure," I nod. "Now go!" I order as I push her toward Alex. He's disappearing into the massive log house by now, and she's going to lose sight of him if she doesn't hurry the fuck up.

"Don't do anything stupid," Sloan warns as she excitedly skips off, following Alex into the house.

Alone and cold, I feel goosebumps pimple along my skin, raising tiny hairs across my arms, and they spread. My breath hitches in the back of my throat, and I find myself scanning the crowd of people.

I know almost everyone here. They're almost all the same people I went to high school with, and if they're not, they're probably married to or dating someone who did. My heart pounds in my chest as my anxiety rises. I'm straining to focus on the faces of the people here.

Across the lawn I catch a brief glimpse of a shadow, but before my eyes can focus, it disappears behind a tree. I take a step forward, determined to get a better look at what I've just seen.

I'm immediately cut off by a young couple running through the lawn, ignorantly playing their adolescent games as though there isn't something lurking in the shadows. I stop dead in my tracks as a ball forms in my stomach, and something in my core tells me I shouldn't proceed. I shouldn't walk into the forest where other partygoers won't notice me if someone snatches me into the woods.

Shaking my head, I curse at myself under my breath.

Fucking stupid.

What would possess me to think it's okay to wander into the woods by myself? I turn, redirecting. The warmth of the house embraces me as I step through the open sliding glass door. The chill I had been feeling seems to fade as I step closer to the alcohol.

"One more won't hurt," I whisper so quietly no one else will hear me. "Take the edge off," I encourage myself.

Lifting the thick ladle from the bowl, I clumsily pour the mixture of liquor and fruit punch into a clear cup. The red liquid spills out from the ladle, covering the sides of my cup with sticky juice.

"Need some help?" a male voice murmurs from behind me. He's so close I can feel his breath puffing against my ear.

Raising a brow, I turn to meet a very drunk Jonah. I bring the cup to my lips, slowly drinking down its entire contents before answering his question. "No," I sigh as I turn back toward the punch bowl, desperate for seconds.

"You shouldn't be near me. If Sloan catches us, she'll never forgive me."

"But, Sloan isn't here, is she?" he smiles the sloppiest smirk I've seen from him. "She went to the back of the house with that Alex fellow a few minutes ago, and judging by the way they passed by me, they won't be back for a while."

"Still," I say as I rotate back, meeting his half-shut eyes. "We need to stop doing this. It's not healthy for either of us to stay wrapped up in something that'll never go anywhere."

Jonah takes a step toward me, quickly closing the distance between us. "You know what's not healthy?" he asks, whispering against my cheek. "Denying your body its… needs."

Gag. Okay.

I wouldn't consider Jonah one of my "needs," but I can't help but squeeze my thighs together at the thought of being satisfied tonight. The alcohol making its way through my veins makes my decision that much easier.

Fuck it.

"Make it quick, and don't let anyone see us," I say before I've thought the words through enough to truly understand the meaning behind them.

"Deal," he winks, snatching my wrist away from the punch bowl as I go back for thirds.

I drop the cup, and the little bit of liquid I managed to pour into it spills over the expensive-looking tablecloth, but I don't have time to clean it off as he drags me away, leading me toward a set of stairs.

Jonah leads me through the house, and as I follow him, I find myself forgetting about Sloan. She's preoccupied with Alex, and I deserve a little bit of a release. We snake through a maze of hallways, eventually stopping at an open door at the end of the hall.

I peer inside. It's dark, but I can see what looks like a guest room. There's a bed, and that's really all I care about at this point. My buzz has surpassed what I originally intended, and I'm rapidly approaching my blacked-out alter ego.

We step inside and I lazily close the door behind us. I don't hear it click shut, but I don't care when Jonah's lips crash into mine, nearly knocking me off my feet as we stumble toward the bed. His tongue assaults my lips, lashing out at them as he pries them open. I allow them to part, and he slides into me, dominating my entire mouth.

Jonah is quick to release his zipper, tugging his cock free as he slams me not onto the bed but against the wall. My clit is pulsing with anticipation as he strokes himself, pushing his cock to be as hard as it possibly can before hiking my skirt up over my hips.

Our kiss deepens, and he's pressing into me so hard that it almost hurts. He's so drunk he can't hold his own weight, and he's using me as support.

His hands slide between my thighs, searching for the pooling heat I have waiting for him.

"You're so fucking wet," he moans out as he slides his fingers over my pussy, spreading his arousal over his hand before slipping three fingers inside me.

"Ahh," I cry out, caught off guard by his sudden roughness and the sharp pain I feel from him entering me so quickly.

"You like that, don't you?" Jonah presses into my ear. "You love it when I spread your wet pussy across my fingers and fuck you with them."

"Yes," I moan as he begins pumping his fingers in and out of me, stretching me wider as he goes. I relax at his touch, trying to enjoy the feeling of being so full, but Jonah's sloppy execution leaves me cringing more than anything.

He grows bored quickly, pulling his fingers out from me. He strokes his cock a few more times, then throws my leg over his arm as he lines himself up against me. I'm standing on the tip of my toes, trying to be tall enough to take his cock to the fullest extent, which isn't much, but I keep reminding myself it's not about size. It's about how he uses it.

Jonah's mouth is back on mine as he shoves himself inside me, filling me as deeply as he can before pulling back out, then slamming back into me with enough force to crack the wall behind me.

He picks up the pace before I can really adjust to him, but I wiggle under him, repositioning myself better as he keeps going. Jonah's breath picks up, and a whiny noise escapes his lips with each thrust. It's somewhere between a porn star moan and a dog that needs to go outside, and that's when I realize Jonah isn't anything more than those two things.

He likes to fuck, but his primary goal is getting himself off. He acts like he cares about what I want for a split second, occasionally, but always reverts back to getting what he wants.

My needs are never met, and that's one of the many reasons I left him to begin with.

Even in this drunken state, Jonah can't pleasure me in the way I deserve. In the way I need.

He's sloppy, selfish, and truly inexperienced, even though we've fucked a thousand times. He's vanilla.

His whiny bitch noises increase with his speed, and I'm doing everything I can to keep the best poker face possible. My back slams into the wall repeatedly as he cries out into my cheek, sweating as he thrusts.

Jonah pulls out, suddenly releasing me from his hold. My body relaxes away from the wall. His leg kicks out as he wraps his hand through my hair, forcing me to my knees before him. Drunk and way too slow, I'm too late by the time I realize what he's doing.

Cock in hand, Jonah is furiously rubbing his hand across his dick. His head tips back as he bites his bottom lip, furrowing his brows as his ejaculation rises.

I open my mouth to protest, trying to push myself to my feet, but I'm too drunk to use my limbs. Jonah immediately busts his load, shooting it all over my face and my open mouth.

I squeeze my eyes shut as quickly as I can, but my eyelashes are already coated in his cum. Jonah cries out, squealing with delight as he ejaculates all over my face.

"Are you fucking kidding me?" I gasp, opening my mouth for air as he finishes. My nostrils are clogged with his sticky white jizz.

"What?" he smirks as he tucks his cock away, zipping himself back up before turning to leave. "Thanks for that," he winks before quickly disappearing through the door we came in through.

Stunned and in a spinning state, I sit there, dazed for a moment.

That bastard just came all over my face, ruining my make-up and my hair, and now I have to go out there and face not only all those people, but my best friend, who will immediately notice my change in cosmetics.

I'm so fucked, and I'm so fucking stupid for thinking this way is a good idea to begin with. Fuck alcohol and the liquid courage it gives me to do the most fucked up shit.

"Fuck!" I yell out, frustrated with how my night is going.

I grip the bed beside me for support, then raise myself off the ground with a face full of cum. I walk toward the door, then peek into the hallway to make sure no one will see me.

It's clear, so I silently make my way down the hallway, checking each closed door to see if there's a bathroom behind it. It takes a few tries, but on the fifth or sixth door, I open it to find a small powder room fully equipped with fresh towels.

Perfect.

* * *

After doing my best to clean myself up and save what I could of my makeup, I head back outside to find Sloan. She's probably done with Alex by now and wondering where I'm at.

I grab two shot glasses filled with clear liquid as I pass by the drink table. Jonah sobered me up far more than I had planned on being this evening, and I can feel my anxiety returning as I approach the door leading to the yard.

A frigid breeze expands in my lungs as I step outside, filling me with the same ghostly chill I've been feeling the majority of the day.

I search the yard a few times, aimlessly walking with my shot glasses. I can't find her, so I decide to shoot back the glasses before I spill any more of the precious liquid inside. They look like they're the same, so I mentally prepare myself to take them one after the other without a break.

Breathing out, I calm myself as I stare at the glasses.

"Go," I quietly encourage myself.

I don't hesitate to bring the first glass to my lips, throwing it back as quickly as I can. It burns like hell going down, but I immediately force the second shot down before I have a chance to back out.

I cringe, scrunching my face as the burn momentarily intensifies, then subsides, leaving a faint raw feeling in my throat.

While I wait for Sloan, I decide I'll observe the apple bobbing going on in the middle of the yard. It's decently dark outside, so I don't understand why now is a good time to go apple bobbing, but I have to admit it's pretty funny to watch a group of drunk people shove their faces into the water, violently sloshing around for a chance at grasping an apple between their teeth.

I watch for a few minutes, and during that time, I feel the effects of the two shots I took begin to kick in. The fire crackling on the other side of the apple bobbing seems to burn brighter, blurring my vision further.

"It's your turn, Cara!" someone yells from the crowd of drunk apple bobbers.

My liquid courage is doing its job, and I don't hesitate to join in on the fun. Fucking up my make-up in the apple bobbing will be a great cover up for Jonah coming all over my face. I approach the deep tank of apples, and I eye the bright green apple I'm going to target.

I hate green apples, but this one will give me the best chance at coming out of this successful.

Leaning back, I inhale one last time before shoving my face down in the apples, trying to get my face just wet enough to mess up my mascara, but not wet enough to damage my curled hair more than it already has been.

I struggle briefly, falling left and right as I bob around. This is a lot harder than it looks, and I'm starting to feel like my mouth is simply too small for this game.

Rising back up, I'm about to tell everyone about the conclusion I've just come to, but a hand forces me under the water, submerging my entire head beneath the surface.

My arms flail around me as I try to fight back, but I'm too disorientated and panicked. I accidentally inhale, sucking in a mouthful of water. I can't breathe, and I feel like I'm drowning. I'm helpless in this moment, completely vulnerable and at the mercy of the hand forcing me down.

The hand releases, and I jump backward, coughing and gasping for air as I try to stabilize my stance.

The sound of Jonah's laugh fills my ears, and my blood instantly begins to boil.

"What the fuck?" I shout, nearly in tears as I try to catch my breath.

Water drips down my hair, soaking my white top so much it becomes translucent.

"Calm down," Jonah spits. "It was a joke."

Fuming, I glare at him. "That wasn't fucking funny, Jonah. You were drowning me."

There's a sly grin in his face. "What can I say? I like forcing you to your knees," he winks before turning, once more disappearing from my view before I can give him a piece of my mind.

I am so never fucking him again. I'm done this time. He's taking things too far.

My hair keeps dripping, so I step away from the water tank to ring it out. As I step away from the tank I find myself locked in a trance, staring directly across the bonfire burning in the middle of the yard.

Beyond the fire is what I believe to be the shadow I saw earlier. A man.

He's dressed casually, but there's a scarecrow mask resting over his face. I can't see his eyes, but I feel them. He's facing me directly, and I know he can see me watching him.

Chills run along my spine, and I strain to catch a better look at him, but the roaring flames in the fire make it hard to see.

"What happened to you?" Sloan gasps from behind me, grabbing my shoulders to assess the situation.

"I…," there's hesitation in my voice. "I went apple bobbing, and I fell in."

Unsatisfied with my answer, Sloan says, "You fell in?"

"Yes," I breathe, turning away from her to get a better look at the masked man through the flames, but he's gone.

Chapter Six
RHETT

Anger is an emotion I am well versed in thanks to the life I've been forced to live and the things that have happened during it, none of which amount to the anger coursing through my body in this moment. Confusion mixed with a rage stronger than I've felt before courses through my veins.

How could she let him touch her? I thought we both felt something in our moment at Rustic Roast.

After watching Jonah touch my girl through the crack in the door, I pity anyone who gets in my way tonight. I watched the fucking show Jonah put on. It was pathetic, really, and I could tell by my girl's face she didn't even finish. She wasn't even close. Not that I can blame her. He was probably done before his tiny dick was even inside her.

I twirl my favorite blade between my fingers, remembering the way he pushed her to her knees, and blew his load all over her perfect little face like she was just some slut he picked up at the local bar.

Like she was his.

Tucking my blade back inside my jacket, I pace with my fists clenched at my sides so tightly it hurts.

My rage grows as I replay every second, every sound she made while he was inside her. It took every ounce of self-control in me not to burst in and slit his throat while she watched.

Then maybe she'd see how badly she needs a real man in her life, not some mama's boy who can't even keep it up long enough to please her. She deserves to be devoured, catered to like a goddamn queen, and since Jonah clearly doesn't have it in him or his micro dick, I'll have to do it…

After I make sure Jonah won't have the ability to let down any other women again, ever again.

As if that wasn't enough, when my little nightmare tries to rejoin the party, he has to come fuck that up too, holding her head under the water in the apple bobbing game while he and his buddies laugh. I want to kill him right here and now, in front of every fucker at this party, and the only thing that keeps me from giving in to that need is her. The moment he lets her up and her ghostly eyes lock with mine through the flames, my heart stops beating. I feel seen, exposed, and I can tell by the way her eyes stare back at me, that she feels it too, my little nightmare.

Jonah will get his, though. He thinks it's so funny to touch what isn't his. I'll show him just how funny it can be when I carve a permanent smile into his face, and my girl will see what happens when she lets others touch what belongs to me. She will learn her lesson.

Sloan finds her in the crowd and is visibly surprised to find Cara soaking wet. She appears to be concerned for her friend once again, and they exchange words through drunken motions. My girl is so drunk she can barely keep her eyes open, and Sloan doesn't look far behind.

They return to the house together, and I'm hypnotized by each sway of my girl's hips.

The girls drink heavily for well over an hour before they stumble into the street, searching the line of cars for theirs.

My little nightmare is still somehow carrying her strappy silver heels along in her hand, clinging to them as they smack against her tightly toned legs.

"I already called us an Uber," Sloan mumbles as she trips over a pebble in the gravel.

Perfect.

I walk past them, stopping at a small black car parked down a ways from them. Leaning against it, I pull out my phone. Opening the browser, all it takes is a few simple codes to have the cab app on my phone and have access to everything I need. I cancel the cab Sloan called and quickly tuck it back into the pocket of my leather jacket.

Pushing myself off the car, I head back towards the party in search of a different kind of prey, the one who won't notice a set of car keys missing. With how drunk these idiots are, it should be easy picking.

I stick to the people outside, striding across the vast lawn of wild grass, toward the fire pit by the water. A few people are passed out against wooden logs around the flames, some are too distracted making out to notice me, and others are too zoned out in the flames to care what's happening around them. A totally different vibe than the party happening over in the house. As I make my way past them, I trip but manage to save it and stay on my feet.

"What the fuck," I curse through my mask with clenched teeth. When I look down, I find a guy dressed in a yellow sponge costume passed out in the grass. My head falls back as I inhale deeply, doing my best not to lose control.

Once I'm calm, I reach down, searching his pockets for keys. If he slept through me tripping over him, this isn't going to wake him. In his right pocket, I find some pre-rolled joints tucked away inside a zip-lock baggie.

Cocking a brow, I tuck them inside my jacket with my blade. I might need those later. Sliding my hand into his left pocket, I find a neon pink lighter, a condom, and a set of keys. Thank fuck.

With the sponge's keys in hand, I jog back toward the rows of parked cars and press the button on the key fob. The lights on a small silver Honda Civic light up a few cars away, so I run over and climb in.

Taking off my mask, I search the backseat for something to change into. As luck would have it, I find a red hoodie. Sliding out of my jacket, I toss it to the passenger floor with my mask and pull the hoodie over my head. It smells like shit, but it will have to do.

Pulling out my phone, I bring up the cab app and enter my codes. I type in the make and model of the car I just borrowed before sending a text to Sloan's phone through the app, letting her know their driver has arrived before starting up the engine and backing out of the spot to make my way over to where I left my girl waiting.

When I pull up beside them, it's obvious they're feeling the full effect of the night chill, even with the insane amounts of alcohol coursing through their veins. They waste no time climbing in the back of my new car. My girl staggers in first, taking the seat behind mine as Sloan slides in beside her.

The car immediately fills with her vanilla cinnamon scent. My eyes flutter, rolling back as I inhale deeply, taking a hit of what's mine.

"Eleven October Lane," my little nightmare stammers.

I turn my head back to her, acting like I didn't already know her address. I know exactly where we're going. Her once-perfect makeup is smeared all over her gorgeous face, and her skin is flush and pink from the cold. This is the closest I've been to her all night, and she's even more perfect than I remember.

"Heyyy, I remember youuu," she smears her words together, giving me a taste of the alcohol on her breath.

Sloan is quick to try and hush her with uncoordinated hands while giving me an apologetic look. I offer her a smile and nod before turning the car down the gravel road and back into town.

The girls are quiet most of the drive, sliding in and out of consciousness as the alcohol takes a deeper root. There's an occasional moan that slips from my girl's lips as she fights sleep, and it has my cock twitching beneath my pants.

After a short ride, I pull up to Eleven October Lane and find the black gothic-style Victorian house I'd been studying on satellite images earlier. The Halloween décor catches my eye, and I can't help but imagine how much effort she put into sprucing up her yard.

I carry both girls down the pathway leading to the porch, then up the steps covered in jack-o'-lanterns that have been long blown out. Sloan fumbles for her keys when I set her in front of the door. She's slightly more coherent than Cara as she unlocks the door. I scoop my barely conscious little nightmare up in my arms, carrying her through the doorway and into the heated house. I head into the large living room with my girl in my arms and Sloan hanging onto me for support. When we reach the couch,

Sloan kicks off her shoes and grabs a throw blanket off the arm.

"You're strong," my girl mumbles. "Can you carry me everywhere? So I don't have to walk ever again? Imagine… Oh, you should come to the party tomorrow. You can carry me around."

"Oh my god, yes, can you carry me around too?" Sloan slurs as she drunkenly plops down on one corner of the large L-shaped couch.

"Yeah? What party is that?" I ask with a smirk, curious about what my little nightmare has planned for Halloween Night as I lay her down carefully on the other end of the couch.

"It's at the pumpkin patch. You have to come! It will be so fun…" she mumbles as she curls up into a ball and dozes off.

Her friend doesn't last long either, passing out on the opposite side of the couch. Grabbing a thick blanket from the back of the couch, I cover my girl up before sliding my phone from my pocket.

Pulling the protective case off, I pop out three small micro-cameras and place one on the shelf next to her hallway, making sure it allows me to view the whole main floor of the house. I slip into the hallway, find the stairs, and quietly sneak up.

When I reach the top I find a bathroom, a guest room, and my girl's room. I slide the creaky door open and step inside. Her heavenly scent of vanilla and cinnamon is stronger here than anywhere else, and I want to fucking bathe in it.

I place a camera on a picture frame she has hanging on the wall, pointing it at her vanity and closet so I never miss a chance to watch my girl get ready for me. With the camera secured, I begin to leave the room, not wanting to dwell any longer. My schedule is fully booked tonight, and I've got plans with Jonah.

Turning to leave, my eyes fall to the ground, where I notice a pair of black lace panties. Bending down, I pick them up and bring them to my nose, inhaling her sweet scent.

Fuck.

My cock hardens instantly.

She even smells like mine.

She left these here on purpose.

She wanted them to be found.

"Such a naughty girl," I smirk, thoroughly enjoying this game my girl is playing with me.

Once back on the main floor, I place my last camera by the front door, allowing me to see who comes and goes before making my way back to my borrowed car.

With my girl safely passed out on her couch, and cameras stashed around, my thoughts return to Jonah, and his treatment of my girl tonight. Sticking the keys in the ignition, I turn over the engine and grip the steering wheel tightly in my hands… hands that will soon be coated in his blood.

I head back towards the party, grinning with feral excitement as my eyes land on my discarded mask on the floor. I have a hot date tomorrow night, and I'm in need of a new costume.

Arriving back at the party, the music is still blasting, but most people have cleared out. I park the small Honda in the lot and turn it off, leaving the keys in the ignition before grabbing my jacket and mask. I pull the jacket on over the borrowed hoodie and slide my mask over my head before stalking off toward the house. I scan the crowd with a predatory focus, sorting through the few remaining people in search of my prey, but unlike my little nightmare, this prey I don't plan to keep.

Chapter Seven
RHETT

After a few minutes of walking around the party, I find him in the kitchen, chatting up some blonde in a sexy cop costume. He's leaning against the large marble countertop, and she's hanging off him like a cheap accessory. Being the pathetic little shit he is, he's eating it up, fueling his ego like he didn't already disappoint one girl tonight with his micro dick and middle-school sex skills. The fact that he has the balls to be already entertaining another chick after treating my girl the way he did, using her the way he did, pisses me off.

I press my back against the wall nearby, crossing my arms over my chest while I watch and wait for my chance to strike.

It doesn't take long.

As if sensing how much of a scumbag Jonah is, another girl pulls her away from him, keeping her untrusting eyes locked with his. I grin, thankful I won't have to waste another two minutes of my life watching him plow through a second girl tonight.

Clearly annoyed by the cockblocking friend, Jonah lifts his pumpkin mask over his head and storms outside, away from the crowds of people and towards the fire pit. He sparks up a joint, and its scent travels in the cold wind behind him, hitting my nose and giving me an idea of how I want to play with him.

He lowers himself to a log beside the fire upon my approach. I decide I no longer need to keep myself hidden in the shadows. My heart races with anticipation and excitement to teach dear Jonah here what happens when we touch things that don't belong to us.

His head turns in my direction as I meet the heat from the flames, and he offers me a nod as he tokes. Sitting down beside him, I stretch my legs out towards the flames, welcoming the way its heat instantly relieves my toes from the night's chill.

"What a fucking night," he chuckles as he kicks his boot around the damp grass.

"Tell me about it," I reply, sliding my mask over my head.

I pull out the zip lock of joints I found earlier on the passed out sponge and rest one between my lips as I spark it. I inhale deeply on it, filling my lungs with the sweet marijuana smoke before exhaling and passing it to Jonah. He takes it and puffs on it a few times before returning it.

"Where are you from? Don't think I've seen you around here before," he adds.

"I was invited," I say coolly.

A coy smirk forms on my face as I inhale on the spliff. My eyes are fixated on the fire as visions of my girl and what he did to her tonight fill my head. I pass it back without taking my eyes off the flickering tips of the dying-out flames.

Once he takes it, I slide my hand into my jacket, gripping the handle of my blade tightly. He hits it, nodding his head at my bullshit story like a gullible puppy, but as he makes to pass it back, he drops it.

We both bend over to pick it up, but he reaches it first, and as he moves to sit back, I bring my arm up and under him, catching him off guard. My blade pierces through his soft flesh, and his chest bone crunches under my fist as I bring the blade home on my target, on my prey.

Slowly, he lifts his bulging eyes to mine. His body stiffens, and the joint slips from his fingers to the ground. I pull the blade from his body and shove it back in. Two, three, four times, mimicking the squeaky sounds he made when he was fucking my girl as his warm blood drips down the blade and onto my hands.

He grips my arm tightly, his last attempt to free the blade that's currently buried deep into his abdomen. I smile down at him, finding his efforts amusing as his face floods with confusion. I could overpower this piece of shit any day, and while I usually get a kick out of the chase, no predator complains about an easy kill. Jonah may be a little bitch, but I still expected at least a small fight from him.

He tries to speak, to beg, but blood leaks from his mouth, making it impossible. Gurgling, sputtering words slip from his lips as I slowly pull the blade out one last time. I release my hold on him, letting him fall to the ground as he wraps his arms around his torso in an attempt to slow the blood oozing from his body.

He stumbles around. His pumpkin mask slides off his head as he chokes on his own screams for help until his legs give out and he falls to the ground with a thud. Gasping, his wide eyes scan our surroundings, searching for someone, anyone, to help him.

"No one is coming," I grin, prompting his terror-filled eyes to snap to mine. "They're all too drunk to even know what's happening, and, well…" I pause, bringing my blood-coated hands to his face. "At a Halloween party, no one thinks twice about seeing a guy covered in blood."

Panic takes over as he begins to hyperventilate with the realization of just how true my words are. Even now, he knows it's over for him, and if by some miracle, someone did come to his rescue, I'd take them out too.

No one will keep me from what is mine, from what belongs to me. Jonah made the mistake of touching what didn't belong to him, and because of that, he had to pay.

His life is mine to take.

His final breath is mine to witness.

"You're wanting me to just stop, aren't you? Wishing I'd hurry up and get it over with," I smirk as I pick the joint up off the ground and take another hit before I continue. "Yeah, my girl wished for that too when you had your pathetic little cock inside her. Couldn't you tell how bored she was?" I laugh. "She was silently begging for it to be over with. Being a one-pump chump is the only favor you did for her tonight. But, anyway," I pause for dramatic effect. "Don't worry too hard. I was sure to puncture all the important organs. It will be over for you soon."

He's squirming around on the ground, drowning in his own blood as he begins to die.

"Normally, I'm a predator who enjoys playing with his prey, but lucky for you, I'd much rather get this over with so I can get back to my girl."

I stand over him, watching the blood trickle from his body and paint the wet grass beneath him a dark crimson color that shines under the moonlight. I hit the spliff again, basking in the glory as his struggle slows and his eyes empty of any remaining hope. The clouds of heated breath in the frigid air grow smaller and smaller until there's nothing, and a single tear glides down his cheek.

My head falls back, and I flick away the spliff as I take in a deep breath, letting the iron-rich air of tonight's kill fill my lungs. Killing has always been an outlet for me, but none of my victims have brought me the relief that Jonah's death has. Even being a simple and easy kill, the satisfaction of knowing he'll never touch my girl again makes it so much better.

Now, Cara is mine, and only mine. She may not fully know it yet, but she will, and she'll have no choice but to accept it.

The urge to do something thoughtful for my girl hits me. After all, she deserves to be spoiled, and I know just what to do for her. Something my little jack-o'-lantern connoisseur will appreciate.

Bending down to Jonah's still-warm corpse, I grab a handful of his blonde hair in my bloodied fist and lift his head off the ground. Bringing my blade to his throat, I run it across the pale flesh. I hack away, cutting through muscles, bones, and tendons until his head is freed from his lifeless body. Any remaining blood leaks out as I stand, his hair still clenched tightly in my fist as I suspend his head in the air before me.

His mouth hangs open, and my shoulders shake with a silent laugh as I envision my girl finding her gift. She is going to love this. My little nightmare.

Eager to get to work on my gift, I toss Jonah's head to the ground, watching it roll away from the dying fire through the long grass. Grabbing his ankle, I drag his body to the rocky shore of the lake. My eyes scan the surface of the water, trying to gauge its depths, but it's impossible in the dark. I pick up some of the rocks, placing them in the deep pockets of his black trench coat, and kick off my boots. Once again, grabbing his ankle, I slowly make my way out into the lake, dragging Jonah's headless body behind me. I swim out as far as I can in the near hypothermic water, his rock-filled pockets weighing me down before I let go of him, allowing his body to sink to the bottom of the lake.

I waste no time swimming back to the shore. Pulling my boots back on over soaked socks, I waltz my way back over to the fire and scan the area for any evidence. My eyes land on Jonah's pumpkin mask, and I smirk as I bend down to pick it up. I slide my scarecrow mask off my head, tossing it to the dying fire before sliding into Jonah's. I grab his head. His once blonde curls are now riddled and caked with blood, and I hold it up in front of my face, making eye contact with him as he stares at me through bulging eyes.

"Thanks, Jonah. I needed a new costume. I've got another party to attend and a whole new kind of prey to chase."

Cocking my head to the side, I contemplate what kind of spooky design I should carve into his flesh for my girl. Lowering myself to one of the logs by the fire, I pull out my blade once more and begin carving out his eyes. Starting with the right one, I jab my blade into his voidless eyeball, popping it out of its socket as strings of tendons and nerves follow behind it. I toss it in the fire before doing the same to the left eye.

I decide to mimic a classic jack-o'-lantern, only carving out his nose and eyes before bringing my blade down to his mouth. Staying true to my promise, I carve Jonah the perfect permanent smile into his flesh. Holding his head up, angling it in the light provided by the fire, I smile, proud of my work. Even though my carving skills don't measure up to those of my girl, I didn't do too badly.

My heart pumps with excitement and anticipation to show her the gift I've made her, a gift unlike anything she's ever had. She's going to love it, I know it.

Satisfied, I tuck my art project under my arm and make my way over to my bike. With my new mask and Jonah's head safely secured in the storage bag on the back of my bike, I climb on and slide my helmet over my head, start up the engine, and pull onto the gravel road, racing back into town.

Walking into my condo, I drop the bag with Jonah's head by the door and go straight for the shower, desperate to wash the remaining blood from my skin.

I scrub myself with a bar of soap as the scalding water pours over me, washing any trace of Jonah down the drain. When I'm finished, I shut off the water, and step into the steamed-up bathroom. I snag a towel from the hook by the door, wrapping it around my waist as I make my way out to my desk, and turn on all my monitors.

Pulling out my chair, I sit down, and type in the codes to the cameras I placed in my girl's house, quickly bringing them up on my screen. The girls haven't moved. They're both still passed out cold on the couch like I left them.

Good.

I zoom in on my girl, getting a better look at her perfect tits rising and falling with each breath she takes.

"Get a good night's sleep. You're going to need it," I whisper, brushing my knuckles across her cheek on the screen. "Tomorrow, little nightmare... Tomorrow you are mine."

Chapter Eight
CARA

My head is pounding so hard it feels as though there's someone drumming beneath my skull. No matter how much light I block out, it's not enough.

I'm hungover, and I'm feeling every sip of alcohol I took last night.

Sloan's head is on the opposite side of my couch, and she has spent the last ten minutes stirring in her sleep; her body fights the rays of midday sunlight creeping through the windows. We're both still wearing our costumes from the party last night, and to be honest, I'm not even sure how we got home.

After being nearly drowned by Jonah in the apple bobbing tank, I decided more liquor was the easiest way to escape my looming anxiety, and boy did it work. Sloan and

I took shots of vodka while seated in massive oak chairs placed around the bonfire. I lost track of how many times we slammed back our little glasses, but it was too many.

Way too many.

Rolling to my side, I feel around between the cushions in search of my phone, eventually finding it on the back of the couch. I tap the screen, and it lights up with a time of 2:37p.m and a text from Jonah.

SORRY ABOUT LAST NIGHT. HOPE YOU'RE NOT TOO MAD AT ME.

I groan, frustrated, as I think about how long he held my head beneath the surface of the water. And not only that, but he thought it was absolutely hilarious. What kind of sick fuck thinks publicly drowning their ex at a Devil's Night party is funny? Apparently Jonah.

It's time for him to find someone else to sink his pudgy little cock into. I've had enough of him and his selfish fucking. My vibrator does a thousand times more work than he does in the three pumps he manages to get in before busting his load. Not only can't he last, but the noises that he makes force me to fold internally, crumpling into a tiny piece of paper while I wait for him to come.

Sex shouldn't be like that. It's time for bigger and better dicks.

I dim the brightness on my phone and then scroll aimlessly for a few minutes while I wait for Sloan to wake. Eventually, she does, and I can immediately tell her hangover is just as bad as mine. Before I can say anything, she's on her feet and running toward the bathroom.

"Oh, fuck," she wails as she sprints at full speed, jumping over the shoes we left in the middle of the floor after we got home.

Being the good best friend that I am, I don't hesitate to leap off the couch, following her to the bathroom so I can hold her hair while she vomits. "Don't puke on the rug," I warn as I pull her bright red hair back and away from her face. I use the thick black scrunchie on my wrist to secure it to the back of her head in a messy bun.

"Than-" she's cut off by a revolting gag before she unloads the contents of her stomach into my toilet bowl.

"You're welcome," I sigh as I stand behind her, averting my eyes from the rank mixture of tequila, vodka, and what looks like chips.

We must have snacked on some at the party last night because we sure as hell didn't make it farther than the living room couch as soon as we got home.

Running my fingers through my hair, I ask, "How did we get home? I can't remember anything."

Sloan shakes her head as it hangs lazily into the toilet. "I don't know. The last thing I remember was when you went back to the apple bobbing tank for redemption. It was game over after that."

We burst out laughing, and our laughter echoes through my under-decorated bathroom. Sloan begins vomiting again, and our amusement quickly fades. We sit in silence for a few minutes while Sloan tries to collect herself at the mercy of my toilet.

"Why didn't you tell me about Jonah?" Sloan's voice is quiet, and I sense a hint of sadness.

Fuck.

Caught off guard, I'm not really sure what to say, so I decide honesty will be the best route during the conversation I've been avoiding. "How'd you find out?"

"So it is true," she snaps, eyeing me with bloodshot and mascara-smeared eyes. "One of Alex's friends told me where you disappeared to and who you went with after I couldn't find you last night. Alex didn't last long, so I was surprised when I couldn't find you a few minutes later." She props her elbow up on the rim of the toilet, resting her pounding head in her hand.

She's disappointed, I can tell.

It's not hard for me to read Sloan, considering how long we've been best friends. She probably suspected I was hiding something from her the entire time I was sneaking around with Jonah.

"Jonah and I are done," I declare to her, hoping I can gain back at least an ounce of her distrust. "He came all over my face after we fucked, which messed up my makeup, and when I saw the apple bobbing, I thought it would be a good way to hide how badly he rearranged my makeup, and then Jonah thought it would be funny to pretend to drown me when I was done."

Sloan's head turns toward me, and I see the fire in her eyes. "Jonah, is the reason you spent the night sopping wet? Are you fucking kidding me?"

She's raging for me, and this wasn't the reaction I was expecting from her. My best friend fights for me even when I've shamefully hidden secrets from her.

"I wish I was kidding," I sigh, leaning my back against the bathroom wall. "I blocked his number already this morning after I woke up to an apology text from him. Fuck that guy."

"Fuck that guy," she repeats, cheering me on in my determination to leave behind the baggage I've been carrying around.

We're both quiet for a few minutes while we're lost in thought.

"I'm sorry I didn't tell you. I knew you'd think I was stupid for continuing to see him, but for whatever reason, I couldn't detach myself from him. After last night it feels a lot clearer what I need to do. The decision to block him felt easy."

Sloan rises from the toilet, wiping a glob of vomit from the corner of her mouth. She turns toward me, eyeing me up and down as she says, "I don't think you're stupid. I think what you did is stupid, but you are not stupid. If you had told me, we could have worked through it, and maybe you wouldn't have needed to be held underwater to come to the determination that he's a bad guy."

"Yeah," I nod. "You're probably right. From here on out, I promise to tell you everything. No more secrets."

"Good," she smiles. "Can we eat like shit all day and watch Halloween movies? I can order a pizza if you order us some tacos from that Mexican restaurant we used to eat at all the time."

"Deal," I confirm. "We need to absorb the rest of the alcohol in our systems so we can start fresh tonight. We should arrange a cab ahead of time or find someone to take us home before we get blacked out this time. It's kind of creepy not knowing how we got home last night."

A faint prickle trails up the back of my neck, raising tiny hairs as it snakes its way around my throat. Chills roll down my spine, but I shake them off, dismissing them as nothing more than my body trying to fight off the after-effects of the alcohol.

That's what I hope, at least.

Bonus Chapter
DUAL POV

CARA

The scalding water cascades down my body as I lather up my loofa with my favorite vanilla and cinnamon-scented body wash and run it along my body, washing away the remnants of last night and the lingering alcohol-scented sweat. I welcome the sting the hot water brings, like a deep cleanse of all the things I want and need to forget. There's one thing I can't rid my thoughts of, though, no matter how hot the water gets or how badly it burns. The man from the café. His piercing eyes have left a permanent mark on my soul, one I don't know how to rid myself of or if I even want to.

I've never felt so intoxicated with someone, let alone a stranger, but as thoughts of him cause a familiar heat to build between my thighs, I find I can no longer deny my body the release it's so desperate for. Rinsing the suds from my body, I run my hands through my slick hair, with visions of his cocky smirk filling my head. My body aches for a release, a release Jonah and his selfishness yet again failed to give me.

No surprise there.

Thankfully, I have my trusty vibrator who never lets me down and thoughts of this new mysterious man for inspiration. Sliding the fogged up shower door open, I grab my vibrating wand from the counter as water runs down my arm and drips along the tile floor. With the sounds making it impossible for Sloan to hear it, I flick it on, and find my favorite setting before lowering it to my throbbing clit.

My thoughts trail off to the man at the café and the look in his eyes when I licked the sweet pumpkin cream from my finger. I saw how his large tatted hands clenched around the mug tightly as he watched and I picture what it would be like to have those same hands clenched around my throat as he fucks me. My wand's vibrations course through my body once I find the right spot; I hold the wand to my clit firmly while my other hand braces the shower wall, keeping me balanced while I allow myself to melt in the pleasure.

My ragged breaths increase with the intense sensations along my clit. I find myself wishing the man from the café was here, in this shower with me. I bet he'd never let me walk out of here, not without making sure I finished. I think of those tattooed hands, and how good his thick fingers would feel, pumping in and out of the deepest parts of me. Fuck. My hips buck against the vibrations, forcing me to grip the wall tighter. I startle as Sloan bangs on the bathroom door.

"Bitch! Hurry up! You're taking forever!" She shouts from the other side.

"I'll be out in a minute, calm down!" I add, doing my best to hide my annoyance.

I refuse to let anyone get in the way of me finding my release tonight. I'm not getting out of this shower until I'm fucking spent. I return my thoughts to those piercing eyes and envision them fixated with mine while he fucks me into the most intense orgasm, letting me ride out its wave on his hard cock. I bet he fucks like the devil himself; he's not the gentle type, he's rugged and rough, and right now that's what I want. What I crave. My body twitches with the thought, and I feel my orgasm building with the continued assault of vibrations pressed firmly against my clit. I grind my pelvis against it in vigorous circular motions, inching myself closer, and closer. Until it stops. My vibrator dies.

You have to be fucking kidding me.

Aggravated, I whip the wand against the tile wall. Fuck Sloan for being right. I was too close to the edge to give up now. Lowering my fingers to my pussy, I circle my clit slowly, mixing my arousal with the shower's hot water before sliding two heated fingers inside myself. My head falls back and my eyes flutter shut as I ride my fingers, imagining they're his. I pump them in and out, while my thumb circles my swollen clit. I picture his head between my thighs with his cheeky grin before he brings his tongue over my heat, sucking and lapping in all the right places.

My body shudders as my climax builds. My fingers pumping inside me bringing me closer to my release as my every thought is consumed by this tattooed god.

"Jesus Christ, Cara! Do you even have hot water anymore? " Sloan bitches as she pounds on the bathroom door again.

"I said hold on!" I snap.

I spread my legs apart, lifting my leg to rest on the side of the shower, allowing my fingers to slide in deeper. Closer to where I need them, crave them. Jonah could never hit the spots I crave the most. His dick was too tiny, and he didn't know how to use it. Didn't care to even learn, so long as he got to bust a nut.

But this tattooed man isn't like that. No, I could tell by the smirk on his gorgeous face that he'd have me screaming his name and my legs too shaky to walk on. If his large hands were any indicator to how big his cock is, he would ruin me, both inside and out. I pick up the pace, fucking myself with my fingers hard and deep. Moans slip from my lips as I near the edge, closer and closer until I'm falling. My body quivers beneath the steaming water causing my back to slam against the cool tile wall of the shower as my orgasm hits me hard.

I ride the wave, letting myself drown in the release I so badly needed, before slowly sliding my fingers from my slick core. My thoughts trail back to the stranger I just got off to as I bring my cum-coated fingers to my lips and suck them clean.

He'd like this if he could see.

I pictured the look he gave me at the café when his eyes glazed with hunger as I licked the cream from my fingers. He wanted me then and there, and I'd have let him take me, too. The thought alone has my pussy fluttering all over again. It's a hungry bitch, and it's starving for this man. I cup my hand over my pubic bone firmly, and begin grinding against it. In my head he's watching. In my head he's touching himself too. Stroking his hand along his thick hard cock, watching as he bites down on his full bottom lip.

Bang. Bang. Bang.

"Bitch! I swear if you don't get the fuck out of there right now, I will come in there and drag your ass out here naked! We're going to be late and I cannot have Alex waiting on me again!" Sloan yells as she bangs on the door again.

"I'm almost done! Calm your tits!" I bark as I grind faster, picturing the pure lust hidden behind his cocky smirk, and know I'd do anything to have him look at me like that again. Sadly, men like him don't stick around in Hallow Grove; there's nothing here for them. He was probably just passing through, and I'll probably never see him again unless it's in my thoughts, my dirty thoughts.

Bang. Bang. Bang.

Rhett

Buzz. Buzz. Buzz.

If it isn't Sloan, pounding on the bathroom door like she works for the FBI, it's the constant buzzing of my cell on my desk that's keeping myself and my girl from getting off. She's in the shower, touching herself. I don't have to be a genius to know who she's thinking about while she does it, either. My little nightmare has already made herself cum once, and then she had the nerve to put on a little show, just for me and lick it off her pretty little fingers.

She knew I'd be watching.

She wanted me to see it.

I pump my hardened cock with my hand, watching as she works her pussy just how she likes it. Mentally taking notes of how rough my girl wants it, how she needs it. It didn't take long to find out my girl's a bit of a freak in the sheets, she was bucking her hips on her own fingers like a star cowgirl in the rodeo and all it did was increase the need I feel to claim her tonight.

Precum beads on the head of my cock and I run my thumb through it, spreading it along my shaft as I watch her on the monitors. Wishing it was my fingers she was fucking like that, or my cock. I bet her pussy is tight and perfect just like her. I picture how her perky little tits would bounce, as I thrust up into her. Filling her tight little cunt with every inch of me over and over. Claiming her. Ruining her. She unknowingly became mine in that café, when her smile changed my whole world.

I tighten my grip on my shaft as I continue to pump myself, my eyes fixated on my girl on the monitor and the little show she's putting on for me. I knew she wasn't going to need that vibrator anymore now that she has me. If mental images of me are all my little nightmare needs to come undone, I can't wait to see how she crumbles when I'm the one touching her. Fucking her.

Buzz. Buzz. Buzz.

My phone vibrates on the desk again, pulling me from the delicious thoughts of my girl. I grab it and quickly whip it across the room. I chuckle, finding it amusing how my girl just treated her vibrator in a similar fashion. See, baby, we were meant to be. My cock twitches in my hand as I stroke it faster, matching the rhythm my girl is rubbing her little cunt on the screen. She's doing everything she can to grip on to the wall as the water pours down her inked skin.

My girl is getting closer. The way she's struggling to grip the wall and stand on shaky legs lets me know she's almost there. I quickly grab her stolen panties from my desk, and bring them to my nose. Inhaling her scent as I pump my cock harder, faster. My hand glides over each ridge and vein effortlessly as thoughts of sinking into her pretty pink pussy flood my head, thoughts of her coming completely undone while I'm balls deep inside her as her pussy clenches down on me with her release.

Buzz. Buzz. Buzz.

I sit forward and bring my face closer to the monitor, doing my best to drown out the sound of my phone from wherever it landed. Once I've claimed her tight little cunt, I'll be taking her ass. Every hole will know what it feels like to be filled with Rhett. Marked and claimed by Rhett. Her moans through the speaker hit my ears and I nearly bust at the sound. Fuck. Everything about her is pure perfection. She is my new drug, and I'm ready to get my next hit.

Faster, she rubs herself, her hips grinding on her hand vigorously. Desperate to cum, so desperate it frustrates me I can't be there to give it to her. I shove her panties in my mouth, sucking her sweet juices off the fabric as I jerk myself to her. Fuck, she tastes so good. Smells so good. I swirl the fabric around with my tongue, wanting more, needing more as her moans once again hit my ears. I growl. Fuck.

That's it, you're almost there.

Cum with me, little nightmare.

Let. It. Go.

Her body convulses as she pushes herself over the edge, for a second time. I watch her, with my eyes glued to the monitor as my little nightmare crumbles in the shower with the orgasm. I pump harder, bringing myself closer to the same edge, eager to follow my girl into the euphoric bliss she's drowning in. I stroke faster, her soaked panties in my mouth muffling the guttural sounds that slip from my lips as I watch her ride it out. That's it, baby.

Pulling her panties from my mouth, I place them safely on the desk. My chest rises and falls quickly with each pant as I release my hold on my thickened girth, denying myself the release I so badly need. I swore I wouldn't; I swore the next time I came it would be inside my little nightmare, and it will be. My balls ache, filled with pent up release that I can't wait to pump into her tonight, filling her tight little cunt with my seed. She'll be ruined and marked as mine.

This girl is the heaven to my hell, the drug to my addiction and nothing will keep this addict from getting his fix. I watch on the monitor as my girl turns off the shower and heads out wrapping a towel around her perfect little body. She wipes her hand through the condensation on the mirror as she checks over her face. The effects of her release have her cheeks sporting a gorgeous rosy color making my still hardened cock twitch. She ruffles her damp hair with a towel and I lean forward, closer to the monitor.

Buzz. Buzz. Buzz.

My phone vibrates again. Annoyed, I lift myself from my chair, and tuck myself back into my pants before heading across the room to pick up my phone. Answering, I bring it to my ear.

"What?" I snap. "Got it, I'll be out of here by morning." Hanging up, I head back to my desk, back to the monitors plastered with my new obsession. The small bit of intel I gave my boss gave us a new lead, outside of Hollow Grove. Time to move on, but not before I've made sure she's mine. I cock my head to the side as I fixate on my girl, watching as she goes about her room in nothing but a towel.

Teasing me.

She will be mine.

"Don't worry. I'm coming for you, *little nightmare.*"

Chapter Nine
RHETT

I spent all day at my desk with my eyes glued to my monitors, watching my girl and her friend. They overslept, inarguably due to the high levels of alcohol running through their systems, and the hours I spent waiting for them to wake were excruciating.

I place my fourth to-go cup of coffee from Rustic Roast down on my coaster and pull the panties I found in her room out of my pocket. Bringing them to my face I run my nose along them, inhaling her intoxicating scent as I watch her on my screens.

This is what she wanted, why she left them for me to find.

My girl knows what she's doing to me. I tuck them back safely in my pocket before stretching my sore, stiff body out in my chair. I barely slept. As expected, thoughts of my little nightmare plagued my head all night, which made getting any sleep next to impossible. My phone buzzes on my desk for the sixth time today. The leading agent on the case I'm working is persistent, I'll give him that. Truth is I'm behind on my work. The surveillance I should've been doing on Jose Demarko, the leader of the Don Leon Cartel, has been spent instead watching my girl.

Jose killed my father, murdered him in cold blood twelve years ago, and since joining the CIA I've spent every minute I could working the case. I have spent any chance I can to get a lead, to get something I can use to bring him down, or to kill him myself. For the first time in my life, someone means more to me than revenge for my father's death. That brief connection we shared at the café turned my entire world upside down, and now the only one I care about watching, the only lead I care about, is her. My little nightmare.

I'm like an addict craving his next fix, and tonight's Halloween party is my dealer, serving me the only thing that's going to silence the burning need that has overpowered every fiber of my being.

The girls are moving around the house, getting themselves ready for the party tonight. Sloan is off somewhere that my cameras don't reach, and my girl is sitting at the vanity in her room, getting herself all dolled up for me.

After watching them all day, I know their entire itinerary for tonight. They plan to be at a cornfield just outside of town within the next hour, which will give me the opportunity to make a quick stop at her house and set up my gift.

Leaning forward in my chair, I rest my elbows on the desk, getting an up-close and personal view of my girl as she prepares herself for tonight. Simply knowing tonight is the night, the night she becomes mine, has my cock twitching, and I'm forced to reach down and readjust myself in my pants. My tongue darts out across my lower lip, wetting it as I grip my thickened girth tightly in my hand, my eyes fluttering closed at my own touch as I envision my plans for tonight and how good it's going to feel to finally sink myself deep inside my girl.

Opening my eyes, I turn my attention back to the cameras as a guttural growl slips from my lips. She doesn't know it yet, but she's getting herself all dressed up for me in her sexy princess costume, and I can't wait to claim her.

Shoving my chair back, I stand, bouncing between feet with excitement for tonight as I watch her add the final touches to her costume.

"Tonight, we play," I say aloud, smirking as she tweaks the silver tiara resting on her perfect head. "And I can't wait to show you what I have planned, baby." I watch as she slides her feet into a set of heels, and find myself unable to control the grin that forms on my face with the thought of how much she's going to regret wearing those later. My voice is barely above a whisper as I speak to the images of her on my screens, "I'm going to fucking ruin you, and watching you break for me is going to be the most beautiful fucking show, little nightmare."

When the sun sets, I observe the girls as they make their way through the house, turning off the lights as they head outside and off to the party in a cab they arranged earlier in the day. I grab my leather jacket off the back of my chair, and race toward the door, eager to get over to my girl's house and set up her surprise. I pick up the duffel bag carrying that bastard's carved head that I left by the door last night, and I swing it over my shoulder in a similar fashion to taking out the trash. My chest tightens with anticipation as I tuck the pumpkin mask into the pocket of my jacket.

"Don't worry, Jonah. I'll sport this mask better than you did, and I'll fuck my girl better than you ever did while wearing it." I smirk, staring down at the duffle bag.

I slip out into the dark hallway, locking the door behind me before walking down to where my bike is parked outside. I climb on and start up the engine. My baby purrs under me, sending vibrations coursing through my body as I hit my heel on the kickstand, slide my visor down, and merge into traffic, speeding to my girl's house.

When I pull up to the dark Victorian house I notice the streets are already filled with trick-or-treaters. They're going door to door collecting candy with their parents close behind them. I'm going to have to be careful while I set up my girl's surprise. Turning off my bike, I slide off my helmet, resting it on the seat as I head up the path toward the house. Ghosts float around the bare trees on her lawn, and the bushes are draped with thick layers of cotton spider webs, tiny black spiders carefully placed around them. As I climb the stairs, I find each step is perfectly decorated, and I can't help but feel like my girl did it all just for me.

It's obvious Cara went all out with decorations. I know she does every year; I've seen the pictures on her social media of past Halloweens, and she always goes all out, but this year she really outdid herself. As I continue up the stairs, I find them littered with masterfully carved pumpkins of all different shapes and sizes, with bright-colored faux leaves and tiny sparkling lights wrapped around them. I stop at each step, taking it all in and admiring my girl's work until I reach the top step.

The porch is dark; the only light coming from the tiny lights and the glowing flames inside each perfectly crafted jack-o'-lantern. I find a chair leaning up against the wall on the left side of the porch and drag it over, placing it right beside the large door to her house.

The perfect place to set up my gift.

If it's right by her door, it will be impossible for her to miss. Carefully sliding the duffle bag off my shoulder, I open it up and pull Jonah's head out, placing it on the chair. It stinks, and the bag is definitely garbage now, but as I look over my craftsmanship, I couldn't be more proud. It may not be as good as my girl's jack-o'-lanterns, but I have no doubt she's going to appreciate the hard work and time I put into it.

Just for her. My little nightmare.

Sliding my hand back inside the blood-soaked duffle bag, I pull out the small candle I threw in there earlier and place it inside Jonah's carved mouth. Pulling out my Zippo, I strike it, light the small cotton wick with the flame, and watch as Jonah's pale head lights up, the holes where his eyes and nose once were illuminated by the tiny flicker of fire resting on his stiff tongue. I thought I did a good job carving before it was all lit up, but seeing it like this, seeing the light shine through his carved-out smile, has blood pumping to my cock.

Cara is going to love it, and I can't wait to see her face when she finally sees what I've set up for her. Killing for her is quickly becoming my new favorite hobby; no one fucks with my girl and lives. Jonah is proof of that, and I don't feel guilty for ridding the world of one less scumbag. Besides, she made me do it. She didn't have to let Jonah touch her, not after the moment we shared; she knew she was mine, or I thought she did. Now she'll never be able to forget who she belongs to, and if she does, I don't mind reminding her; it will give me another chance to work on my carving skills.

Pulling out a cigarette from my pocket, I place it between my lips and light it as thoughts of how tonight is going to go flood through my head. I can't remember the last time I felt this anxious about anything, let alone a woman, but my girl is different. She's not like the others, no. Cara saw the dark side of me when she looked into my eyes; I felt it. In that split second, she learned that I am the predator, and she is my prey, but she didn't back down. She wants it. My little nightmare craves the chase just as badly as I do, and well, who am I to deny my girl what she wants?

I inhale deeply on the cigarette, the embers blazing bright orange as I fill my lungs with the intoxicating fumes. I fill the air around me with smoke as I exhale.

"You wanted to play baby, so let's play," I smirk as I toss the butt into Jonah's mouth and head back down the stairs. I pull my helmet down over my head and climb onto my bike, my cock still hard and ready to sink deep into my girl.

Revving up the engine, I flip up the kickstand, taking one last look at my little setup before pulling out of the driveway and zipping off towards the pumpkin patch, towards my little nightmare.

Chapter Ten
CARA

Loud rock music booms through my head, occasionally making me flinch when the bass player goes a little too hard on the stage composed of wood pallets. I hadn't expected a live band to be performing at this party, and I can't decide if I love it or hate it. My hangover screams with each beat, but the gothic side of me adores some good rock. Without being able to hear much other than the music, there isn't a whole lot of talking that needs to be done, and that makes it easier to consume alcohol at a faster rate.

Tonight, I'm drinking to cure my hangover. Tomorrow, I'll deal with the ultimate hangover, but that's in the back of my mind for now. We're here to enjoy ourselves and celebrate my favorite holiday: Halloween.

CARVING FOR CARA

A bonfire blazes in the center of the cornfield, and party goers are mingling everywhere. Most of us have a drink or two in our hands, hand-crafted by the mobile bar set up by one of the caterers in town. On the far side of the field is the pumpkin patch, but there's no light out there and no one has migrated out there yet.

That eerie feeling creeps up my spine once more, prompting me to down the pomegranate cocktail in my hand. I close my eyes as I guzzle it, allowing the full effect of my buzz to set in. I don't know why I can't shake this feeling.

Halloween is full of gore, terror, and fucked up shit, but this feels different. I feel like I'm being watched again, but I can't see anyone watching when I scan the field around me. It's too dark to see beyond the first few rows of corn, which isn't ideal when I'm looking for potential threats.

"Stand in front of me," I suddenly snap at Sloan when Jonah comes into view. "Jonah's here."

Without hesitation, my best friend does as she's asked, blocking me from Jonah's view. "How's this?" she asks.

"Good," I nod. "He's wearing the same costume he wore last night."

Sloan scoffs, laughing louder than she intends to, but the alcohol is beginning to talk for her. "He couldn't find time to buy a different mask? Wasn't there a shop set up outside Rustic Roast? He's the laziest piece of shit I've ever met."

She's being slightly dramatic, but I don't blame her considering what has transpired and been revealed in the last twenty-four hours. She's pissed off at him and wants him away from me just as much as I do.

"We need more drinks," I suggest as I notice both of our cups are now empty.

Sloan's face lights up at the mention of more alcohol. "We'll get more drinks, then we'll look around for new potential fuck buddies."

"Thanks," I smile. "I'm really done with him this time. I didn't deserve to be dunked in the tank last night." As an afterthought, I add, "And his dick is too small anyway."

"I was always worried about that after you showed me one of the dick pics he sent you in high school. Who would take a picture of that and voluntarily show it to anyone else?"

"Someone who delusionally thinks they're bigger than they are, or has convinced themselves it's not how big it is, but how they use it."

She bursts out into a cackle, stumbling as we walk toward the bar. "You're probably right."

Sloan remains by my side for the next couple of hours, never wandering and always keeping a sharp lookout for Jonah, or as sharp as she can be in our intoxicated state. We've already had too much to drink, so we're trying to slow down. We've been standing in a circle of people we went to high school with, chatting about the good ole days and reminiscing on some of the stupid shit we used to do.

I suddenly feel an urgent need to pee, but Sloan is so deep into her story telling I don't want to cut her off to announce to the group I need to pee, so I silently step back, exiting the circle without interrupting anyone.

Quickly finding the porta potties, I'm irritated when I see they're not only all occupied, but there's a line a mile long to get into them. There's no way I can wait that long, so I decide I'll sneak off into the corn to pee. No one will notice me and I'll be back in a fraction of the time.

Glancing around before stepping into the corn for privacy, I make sure no one sees me. The coast is clear, so I disappear into the thick rows of dried corn stocks, desperate to relieve my bladder.

Pin point prickles pimple goosebumps along my forearms as I walk deeper and deeper into the corn. I can't pee within the first few rows because it's too risky, so I keep going against my better judgment. About fifty feet back I decide I'm far enough away. The voices of party goers fade, and all I can hear is the boom of the live band playing.

I pull up my skirt, squatting over a dried mound of dirt as I let a steady stream of urine flow from my body. My eyes roll back with delight as I find instant relief. The sound of mud being made by my pee is interrupted by the steady crunching of boots on brittle dirt.

"Who's there?" I yell into the night, pinching off my stream as I look around. "I'm peeing! Don't come over here!"

My warning is ignored, and the crunching escalates, growing louder by the second.

I squint, straining to see through the darkness surrounding me. The outline of a man comes into view, and my vision adjusts slightly as he comes closer. That's when I see the pumpkin mask and realize it's Jonah.

Annoyed he followed me into the corn and had the audacity to sneak up on me mid-pee, I snap at him, "Get the fuck away from me."

He says nothing as he stands roughly ten feet away, barely visible in the shadows.

"If you don't leave me the fuck alone, I'm going to let Sloan tell the entire town about how small your dick is."

Still, nothing. He's hovering in place, watching me intently behind the mask.

He's acting weird. Really fucking weird, so I keep my verbal assaults coming. "If you could last more than two seconds maybe we would have had more of a chance, but you couldn't, and you never cared about my needs."

Again, nothing.

"Selfish bastard," I mumble under my breath, rising from my squat.

I adjust my skirt back into place, then turn my attention back to Jonah. He's just watching me, being a fucking creep. Pissed off, drunk, and unamused, I stalk toward him with clenched fists, only to be stopped after a few steps.

My heart stops as my breath hitches in the back of my throat.

I was wrong. It's not Jonah.

Whoever this is, is much larger than Jonah, both in height and muscularity. But, why is he wearing Jonah's costume?

A heavy ball forms in the pit of my stomach, sending that anxious feeling rattling through me. My gut is telling me that something is wrong. Very wrong, and I need to get out of here.

"Who are you?" I ask, stalling as I think of a way to get back to the party, back into the public eye, where there are witnesses if this creep tries to kill me.

The man wearing the pumpkin mask chuckles. His laugh is deep, haunting me to my core as he releases it. Waves of chills roll down my spine, and I break out into a cold sweat.

His voice comes smooth and firm, perhaps even sexy in the most wrong of ways. "Run, little nightmare."

Chapter Eleven
RHETT

My little nightmare is quicker than I expected, and watching her frantically run through the tall stalks of corn in front of me sends a thrill up my spine. I fucking love the chase; the false sense of hope she has that she'll get away from me only makes my cock harder. I suspected she would be too smart to fall for the mask. Once I was close enough, it was obvious I wasn't Jonah. Just a stranger wearing the mask of her dead ex, his blood dried and painted across the front of it. I watch her run ahead of me, her screams for help drowned out by the live band I hired to ensure no one would hear her and ruin our plans. I hate interruptions.

I follow her through rows of corn. The dried soil of the field crumbles under my feet in my chase, sending clouds of dust drifting into the night air. It's clear the drinks of the night are having an effect on her as she manages a quick glance back at me over her shoulder. The heels she chose couldn't be any worse for a place like this. Unable to run in them, especially through uneven dirt, makes catching her that much easier. Another thing I'm sure she did on purpose.

My little nightmare plays this game so well.

"Do you really think you can get away from me?" I shout into the night. My heated breath turns to vapors, dissipating into the cold air. She wants me to catch her, we both know it. Even if she doesn't want to admit it to herself. If she really wanted to escape me, she'd have run towards the party, towards the people who would try to help her. Not that they'd stand a chance of keeping me from my prey. Not tonight. Instead, Cara is running farther away from the crowds of people surrounding the bonfire, away from her friends. The farther the chase takes us, the easier it is for me to catch her, and she knows it.

I retreat to the shadows, wanting to make things more interesting. Condensation coats my face from my own breath as I watch my girl through the mesh eye holes of Jonah's mask. She's frozen in the narrow space between the corn, a mix of relief and terror etched into her gorgeously flushed face. She thinks she's lost me. She scans her eyes over the rows of corn, as she backtracks down the path she came from, searching for me. Hidden in the shadows, she passes by me, one step at a time, each one taken cautiously as though she's afraid of alerting me of where she is. Sneaking up behind her, I keep my steps silent, a trick I've learned to do over the years.

Something to the left of her moves along the ground, causing the stalks of corn to sway, and startles her causing her to take off running back the way she came and out of my sight.

Fuck.

I take chase, not wanting to lose her in the dense field. The dry ground makes tracking her next to impossible, the only sign of her being the tiny heel marks that her shoes leave in the dead earth. I trail her through row after row of corn, inhaling her vanilla cinnamon scent as I follow the mark her heels leave behind until I hear her cry out. I pounce into action, pushing stalks of corn out of my way as I rush toward the direction of the sound. A few rows over stuck in the dried dirt, I find her shoe.

I can't help but release a low growl as I close in.

Though I love the chase, it's time for a bit of fun. It's time to give my girl a little taste of what awaits her. Following the mouth-watering scent of my prey, it doesn't take me long to catch up to her. Especially when she's down a shoe and heavily intoxicated. I stalk her through the rows of corn, listening for her panting breaths. She isn't far, I can feel it. I soften my steps, returning to the shadows as I stalk her. Sneaking up from behind, I lace my arm around her, covering her mouth to muffle her screams as my other arm wraps around her waist, roughly pulling her back against my chest.

Just touching her has my cock rock hard and desperate to get inside her, to claim her, but not yet; she still needs to learn what happens when she lets others touch what's mine. Keeping one hand on her mouth, I use my free hand to pull out my blade and bring it to her throat. She gasps and presses up against me so tightly I can feel her heart beating against my chest.

I quickly spin her around so I can get a good look at the little nightmare that's caused such an obsession in me. She barely reaches my shoulders, and as I look down on her, I tenderly brush a hair from her face before slowly running my thumb across her bottom lip.

"These lips would look even prettier wrapped around my cock." My confession causes her to snap her eyes to mine, with a glare filled with so much hate it sends a chill up my spine.

"Don't make a fucking noise, and lay down," I command her. She stiffens, briefly, but does as she's told. She turns to look at me and her ghostly eyes lock with mine through Jonah's mask as she slowly lowers herself to her back on the cold dirt. Looking down on her I know immediately I've never seen anything more beautiful. Cara could be laying anywhere, on anything, and she'd be the most gorgeous fucking thing to walk the earth.

My cock pulses in my pants at her obedience and the look of conflicted defeat that paints her face. I lower myself to her, tracing my blade up and down her tight little body, taking in every inch of her up close. She shakes and turns her head away to look away from me, causing anger to build up inside me. I snap my blade up to her chin, tapping its point against her flesh, forcing her head back in my direction. My eyes rake across her flushed face, damp with sweat from our game. Her mascara is running down her cheeks as I work my way down her face until my eyes fall on her perfectly pouty lips. They're red and chapped from the cold night air, but every fiber of me wants to taste them, feel them against mine.

"Kiss me," I demand.

As if she finds my demand amusing, she spits out a bout of laughter, mocking my request.

"Funny, is it? I have something amusing this blade can do, and I bet it would wipe the smirk off your pretty little face and leave you on your knees, begging for more." I add.

Ignoring my threat, she turns her face farther away.

Accepting her defiance, I bring the blade's tip to the swell of her breast, slicing it through her perfect flesh. A loud hiss escapes her.

"Kiss me, or I'll keep going," I warn one last time.

She turns to face me, her eyes filled with hunger as she slowly raises Jonah's mask just past my lips, keeping the rest of my face covered, before her lips crash on mine in a needy, angry kiss that sets my whole body on fire. She pulls away, and I instinctively grab her tightly by the throat, causing her to gasp as her pulse quickens. Her eyes widen with fear, and her hands clamp down on my forearm in a poor attempt to loosen my grip.

"What's wrong, little nightmare?" I whisper, bringing my masked face inches from her ear. With my free hand, I lift a lock of her hair and bring it to my nose as I inhale her scent.

Fuck, she smells divine. To think fucking Jonah got to experience her, smell her and feel her, it pisses me off. He never deserved her, no one does. No one is good enough for my little nightmare, not even me. That's why I have to ruin her, break her.

With my hand still tightly wrapped around her frail little throat, she whimpers and squirms, but has given up trying to free herself. She looks up at me, her ghostly eyes half opened. She seems almost content. Good.

"Let me go," she seethes, and I can't help but chuckle.

I cock my head to the side. "Why should I? You know you're mine, don't you?"

"Get the fuck off me!" she shouts, as she kicks and squirms in the dirt, knocking cobs of dried corn from their stalks. "Help!" Her shrieks for assistance fall on deaf ears. Everyone is blackout drunk by now or unable to hear her over the live band.

Keeping her pinned down by the throat, I drag my blade down her body, stopping at the tiny skirt she wore for me tonight. I push her skirt up her thighs with the tip of my blade and freeze. My girl has no panties on and with her bare pussy exposed, the moon's glow reflects just how fucking wet she is for me.

"Damn, little nightmare," I breathe. "I haven't even touched you yet, and look how wet you are for me," I whisper with a husky tone. Quickly I bring my hand down hard on her slick flesh to teach her a lesson, the sound of the smack echoes around the field, and the impact causes her to jump. "You came to this party, with all these people, all these fucking men, and didn't put panties on?" I growl, rapidly losing my patience.

Turning my blade around in my hand, I rub the pommel across her pussy in slow circular motions, causing her body to stiffen. I lift my eyes to hers, watching her expression change with her internal battle. It's obvious she likes it; her eyes are hooded with a mix of fear and hunger that gets my cock throbbing. My girl fucking likes this; I knew she would, but I want to push her limits. I want to see how long she plans to fight what we both know she really wants because we both know she wants me to devour her.

Grabbing one of the cobs, I use my teeth to peel off the husk and bring it to her lips. "Suck on it." At first, her expression is one of confusion, but as I press the cob to her lips, panic sets in.

"Fuck you!" she spits before clamping her mouth shut.

"Oh, you will," I reply as my shoulders shake with laughter; her defiance is amusing and arousing all at once, but her eyes can't lie. Right now, there's an internal war happening, and only she and I know about it. Like a secret game we have between the two of us. "You are mine, little nightmare, and you will do as I tell you."

"Yours?" she scoffs. "I'm not yours, you fucking freak. I don't even know who the fuck you are or why you're wearing that mask!"

Gripping my fingers around her chin tightly, I force her to look at me. "Oh, but you are. You are mine, and I will carve my name into your perfect flesh if that's what it takes for you to accept it. You will scream the name Rhett every day for the rest of your life. It may begin in fear, but I can promise you it'll always end in pleasure," I argue sternly. "Now, don't make me hurt you again. We both know how much you like it, but I need you to be a good girl and suck on it like you were told."

"You're sick. Help!" she shouts into the night.

Annoyed, I tighten my grip on her throat, instantly silencing her screams. I once again bring the cob to her mouth and push it through her tightly clamped lips. She chokes as I push it to the back of her throat, and I slowly release my hold on her throat. Lowering my hand between her thighs, I circle her swollen clit with my thumb as I continue to fuck her mouth with the cob of corn. Her pelvis instinctively pushes against my hand, seeking more friction for the release she craves, her moans muffled by the cob of corn in her mouth.

"That's it, baby, you can take it. Show me what that pretty little mouth can do." My cock throbs in my pants, the barbells of my Jacob's Ladder rubbing against my boxers, only heightening my arousal. I grab her hand and place it against my hardened cock, causing a quiet moan to slip from her lips. "Only you can get my cock this hard, little nightmare. Only you," I repeat.

With the cob thoroughly lubed up, I pull it from her mouth and lower it to her center. Her eyes widen, and she digs her hands into the dried soil as she readies herself for what's to come. She watches the cob of corn as I run it through her slick folds, teasing her opening with its bumpy girth. Clearly wanting more, she widens her legs, allowing me better access, and I slowly slide the tip inside her. Her head falls back as her hungry pussy swallows the cob of corn deeper with each thrust. I start slow, wanting to watch her tightness stretch around it, savoring every second of my girl in this moment.

She's completely consumed in the moment, no longer caring who I am or what I'm doing. Fucked up or not, there is only one thing my little nightmare needs, and in this moment, she knows I'm the only one who can give it to her. I pick up the pace, thrusting the cob of corn up and into her tightness faster and harder.

"Look how fucking sexy you are when you're at my mercy." Riding the high of my words, with my fingers now aggressively circling her clit, her body shudders and convulses. "That's right, little nightmare. Cum for me. You know you want to. You know you need to."

"I can't, please," she begs, but it's too late.

She cums, hard and it takes everything in me not to lower my mouth to her pussy and drink in every drop of her release. She moans and cries out, tears streaking her face as I continue pumping the cob of corn in and out of her, her juices dripping down and onto my hands as she rides out her orgasm. When she comes down from her high, I slide the corn out and bring it to my mouth, tilting my mask just far enough away from my face to slip the cob underneath. The sweet taste of her coats my tongue, instantly becoming my new favorite meal. My eyes flutter shut as I suck the cob of corn free from all her juices, refusing to let a single drop go to waste.

When I open my eyes, my girl isn't where she should be. Instead, she's a few feet away, stumbling around the narrow path between the stalks of corn. She wants to play again, I see. Standing, I watch her with amusement as she tries to make a silent getaway. Her legs shake beneath her weight. Add in the traumatic mix of emotions I know I just caused her with the drinks from earlier, and she isn't getting very far.

My chest fills with pride, knowing she has it in her to try.

My girl is a fighter, and I fucking love it.

I tuck the cob of freshly creamed corn into my pocket and head out after her. She hears me coming up behind her and takes off, tripping over a mound of dirt in her path.

I pause, watching her scramble to her feet and take off running away from the party. She wants to be chased. I pull out a cigarette and spark it up, inhaling as I let my girl get a head start. The thrill of the hunt fills my body with adrenaline as I watch the stalks of corn shift and sway as she makes her way towards the pumpkin patch, a private setting for what I have planned tonight. The perfect place to claim my little nightmare, and make sure she knows who she belongs to.

Chapter Twelve
CARA

Cursing at myself under my breath as I run out of the cornfield, I'm fucking pissed off for not only choosing to get this drunk tonight, but for having such a poor choice in shoes, not to mention the fact that I just had a mind-blowing orgasm served to me on a corn cob by a masked man in a corn field. Who wears heels to a cornfield? And who the fuck do I think I am coming all over this man's corn?

Me, apparently, and I'm a fucking idiot.

I want to say I don't want him to catch me, and I don't want this stranger to touch me, fuck me, or even look at me… but something buried deep down in the dark depths of my soul is singing. There's adrenaline coursing through my veins, and I don't think it's all out of fear. There's sexual arousal, as he just proved, and I feel so deeply conflicted right now.

I shouldn't like it, and I shouldn't want it, but there's something deeper going on than I can understand right now. I'm overloaded, and I don't know how to process it.

The cornfield comes to an abrupt end, opening to the widely spread pumpkin patch. Most of the pumpkins are picked over, leaving only a few rotting fruits left in the field.

Rhett isn't far behind me, and he's playing games. He knew I wouldn't make it very far in this drunken state with one heel somehow securely strapped to my foot. It's almost like he planned this and fucked with my shoes.

But, how could he? I was home all day and most of the day yesterday, and this man doesn't know me, or at least I don't think he knows me. He said his name was Rhett, and I don't think I know anyone by that name.

Or do I?

"This is the perfect location," Rhett announces loudly as he exits the cornfield behind me. Throwing his hands up, cigarette puffing lazily from his mouth, he continues, "To claim what's mine."

"I'm not yours," I spit, backing deeper and deeper into the pumpkin patch.

I'm too far away for anyone to hear my screams. I've stupidly run to the far end of the farm, and I know there won't be anyone stumbling out this way. A small part of me feels like I may have done this on purpose, though, separating myself further from safety. Perhaps I'm feeding into his chase.

He laughs in the same hauntingly sexy way he did when he first appeared in the corn. There's something about that voice…

Rhett watches me intently through the mesh eye holes as he takes a step forward. My heart and breathing stop at the same time as I wait, trying to anticipate his next move. There isn't much out here for me to defend myself with, and I've clearly got no weapons hidden anywhere on me.

He takes another step forward.

"Get the fuck away from me," I threaten, picking up a rotting pumpkin as I continue to back away from him.

He matches my pace, stepping toward me with each step I take away. After a few long, drawn-out moments filled with anticipation, he tosses his cigarette, smashing it into the ground beneath his foot as he twists it.

"I can't do that," he says in a chillingly calm manner.

"Why not?" I breathe.

"Because I made a promise to both of us after I saw you walk into the coffee shop with your little redheaded friend." He takes another stride toward me.

He's talking about Sloan. He must have seen us at Rustic Roast yesterday.

"What promise?"

"That you'd be mine and that I'd claim you tonight." Downwind of him, I catch a whiff of his scent: cedar and citrus. "I don't break my promises."

For whatever reason, I don't doubt that. I believe every word leaving his deranged mouth. "I'm not yours," I say in the sternest voice I can manage.

Closing in, he's only ten feet away now.

Doing the only thing I can think of in this moment, I throw the rotten pumpkin at him, and it explodes all over his leather jacket. He stops, freezing in place as he analyzes the damage I've done. I don't hesitate to pick up another pumpkin and throw it at his head as he's caught off guard.

His hands go up, and he begins to block my assaults, but I throw pumpkin after pumpkin, trying to buy myself time while I think up a plan.

But, my mind is empty. I'm void of all ideas, and I'm at a loss for what to do.

He speeds up, sprinting at me full speed before I can even flinch. His body slams into me as he tackles me to the ground. I struggle against him, fighting and kicking, but his heavy body weight is too much for me. He easily pins me to the ground while he pulls pumpkin vines from all around us, making quick work of tying me up.

He pulls on the vines as though they're rope he bought from the hardware store, and he makes a satisfied sound when he sees they don't budge. My hands are tied above my head while my ankles are tied separately to vines on both sides of us, spread wide for him. I try to pull against them, but they only tighten, leaving no room for me to move.

A heat in my core begins to warm when I realize just how stuck and at his mercy I am, and I can feel myself getting wet again. I'm terrified of the man hovering over me, but I'm not afraid for my life.

In the fight, my skirt was hiked up over my hips, and now I'm completely bare before him. Not wearing panties tonight is another thing I'm cursing myself for.

The sound of his pants unzipping hits my ears, and my nipples perk up.

Leaning over me, he brings his face close to mine as he wraps his hand around my throat. "This is punishment for not wearing panties and for fucking Jonah in front of me last night. You are mine, and I will pleasure you however I please. Your body was made for me."

"You're delusional," I whisper into his ear, sending chills down my own spine.

For fucking Jonah in front of him? Was he following me around all night?

My back involuntarily arches as he surprises me, sliding the head of his firm cock against my clit, coating it in my arousal.

"Am I?" he asks, swirling his hardness around my clit.

"Yes," I breathe through unsteady breaths.

He pulls his dick away, replacing it with his large, coarse fingers. His thumb rolls around my clit in circles, and a quiet whimper escapes my lips, turning into a moan as it gets louder with each swirl. Pushing one finger inside me, I cry out as it slides easily.

"Mmm," he growls against my ear. "Am I making you feel good, little nightmare?"

"No," I shake my head, but my body betrays me when I suck my bottom lip between my teeth, biting down as my pleasure builds.

"You're lying." I can hear the smile in his voice. He forces a second finger inside me, pumping me three or four times before filling me with a third thick finger. "You're so fucking wet," he groans into my ear.

Rhett's hand begins to move faster, thrusting in and out as he ramps up the pace. Shaking under the pleasure, I cry out, feeling overloaded with the intensity of the incoming orgasm. His fingers continue to move inside me while he presses his thumb against my clit, applying firm pressure as he goes.

I wiggle against him, desperate for air as I drown beneath his rough touch. He's too fucking good at this. I shouldn't be loving this as much as I am, but I can't help myself. My body is screaming for him, for more of him.

Stars begin to form in my vision as my orgasm goes ripping through me. I scream out into the frigid night, riding the high for as long as his fingers keep moving inside me. My body jerks against him, instinctually riding against his fingers as much as my bounds will allow.

"That's it, baby," he moans between each deliciously dark thrust. "You fucking love this."

As the ecstasy of my orgasm calms, he removes his fingers from my pussy, bringing them to my mouth. "Open," he commands, pressing against my lips.

Remembering his knife and what he did with it the last time I disobeyed a direct order, I open my lips for him.

"That's my good girl," he praises as he sinks his fingers inside my mouth. "Close your mouth, and suck."

I shut my lips around his fingers, flicking and rolling my tongue against his fingers as I suck against him. My eyes flutter back, and I can feel heat building between my thighs again.

"Do you know what you taste like?" he asks, removing his fingers from my mouth when he's satisfied with my work.

I don't answer him, I only stare up at him as he lines his dick up against my traitor of a pussy. I'm more wet for Rhett in twenty minutes than I have been for any other man I've been with.

"Mine."

Chapter Thirteen
RHETT

I watch my hardened cock slide inside her. Her tight pussy swallows each steel barbell of my Jacob's Ladder one at a time like she was fucking made for me. Every inch confirms how mine she really is. I can feel it. No one has ever felt this fucking good, and I know they never will. She fights me, but as the seconds pass and she realizes how good it feels, how good I can make her feel, she begins to let go and allow herself to be completely consumed by the same hunger, the same need I have.

I know she wants it.

Wants me.

Her eyes roll into her head as I sink inside her fully. The vines wrapped around her wrists are tearing at her flesh, sending streaks of crimson blood down her arms, but she doesn't care.

No.

My girl, she likes the pain. She gets off on it. I knew there was a dark side hidden behind the nice girl facade; I knew I could break her, I had to. And now, she's broken. Ruined.

It's what she wanted.

My little nightmare wants this.

She fell right into my trap. Everything I had planned for tonight worked out perfectly. The band I hired made it impossible for anyone to hear her; Sloan is well entertained and won't even notice my girl is missing. Nothing will stand in the way of our night, and nobody will stop me from making her mine. I've waited long enough to get my fix, and she's waited long enough to get the type of affection she needs, the type of affection only I can give her.

I grip her top in my fist as I pause with my cock in the deepest parts of her. A hiss slips through my lips at just how fucking good she feels, how tight her pussy hugs me as it adjusts to my size and girth. Looking down at her, at how good she takes it for me, I couldn't be more proud of my little nightmare. I lace my fingers through the thick locks of her dark hair, now matted with dried dirt and pumpkin leaves, and pull her hair up, forcing her to watch.

"Fuck. That's it, baby. Look how good your pretty little pussy swallows my cock," I growl as I pull out slightly, then thrust myself into her harder. The sweet little crying sounds she makes threaten to make me come undone, each moan laced with pleasure. A silent cry for help hides behind the plea for more, and it fucking gets my blood pumping.

I tug on the top of her little princess costume, pulling it down and freeing her perky little tits of their confinement. Gathering the saliva in my mouth, I spit on them before slapping one. She shivers at the sensation, biting down on her bottom lip as her pussy clenches down on my cock.

At first, I fight the urge to mark her with my bite, knowing it could easily get me caught if she reported me to the local police, but it's useless. I need to taste her, to feel her flesh between my teeth.

Bending down, I run my tongue along the swell of her breast before taking her peaked nipple in my mouth, sinking my teeth into her inked flesh. She tastes like the forbidden fruit, sweet like honey with a hit of spice that makes my mouth water. I wish I could taste her, devour her for every meal.

She shivers at the sensation as a moan slips from her lips, and it makes my dick twitch inside her. I can feel my cock leaking inside her with my impending release.

I let go of her hair, allowing her head to fall back against the dirt as I pick up the pace. My hips roughly crash into her. I watch her, completely enthralled by how good my little nightmare looks when she's taking my huge cock inside her fully. She has more of a hold on me than she knows; watching the supple pink flesh of her pussy clinging so tightly to my hard cock is something I'll never tire of.

When she notices I'm watching her, her eyes flicker with guilt, like she feels she shouldn't be enjoying this. She doesn't want to like it, but she does. My girl fucking loves how I feel inside her, and she wants it. Her face flushes with embarrassment as she turns to look away from me.

Fuck.

I love watching her as she loses the internal battle with her morality. Bringing my fingers down, I flick her right nipple causing her to wince and snap her head back to face me, her eyes fierce and ready to challenge me.

"Eyes on me, little nightmare. There's no one around to watch," I growl, lowering my lips mere inches from hers. "It's just you and me, now let go."

"Fuck!!" she screams. "Fuck, plea—" she whimpers, trembling through the building pleasure.

"That's it. Scream, moan, beg for it to stop when we both know you want to ride this pumpkin, princess," I smirk, finding amusement in the pun as I bring my hand down to smack her other tit.

Before she has time to process the smack, my mouth is over her peaked nipple, pinching it between my teeth. Fear flickers in her eyes as she's forced to watch me have my way with her, unable to stop me with her hands tightly tied above her head.

Sitting back up, I pull the cob of corn I fucked her with from my pocket, and run it up her body as her eyes stay locked with mine. When I reach her lips, tears spill from her eyes, and the hatred in her glare threatens to burn through me.

"Open," I command, my tone stern. Being the fighter that she is, she does her best to avoid it, to keep her head turned away from me. I pause mid-thrust, and grip the hair at the top of her head. A whimper leaves her chest as I force her face back in my direction. I push the cob of corn through her quivering lips as she tries to protest. It hits the back of the throat, her teeth scraping along the rigid exterior as she mumbles pleas around it before choking. Her eyes clench shut, and tears stream down her cheeks as she does everything she can not to gag.

"Fuck," I growl, doing my best to calm myself down. She feels so good, and I've been waiting so long, it takes everything in me not to combust and fill her with my cum.

The sounds of her objections only make my cock harder. My little nightmare grows wetter with each thrust into her, moaning and pushing back into me, moving in rhythm with me. With each thrust, her walls break; one by one they're crumbling, and by the time we're done, the only thing left standing among the ruins of her mind will be me. With each wall that falls, she learns to welcome the pleasure, the pleasure that only I can give her.

She wraps her lips around the cob of corn, locking her eyes with mine as she teases me. My pulse increases as I dart my tongue across my lips, picking up the pace.

Finally, someone who gets me. My girl knows just what kind of games I like to play, and she is so fucking good at playing them. My head falls back and my eyes close as visions of her soft lips wrapped around my cock fill my thoughts, her tongue swirling around my piercings as she sucks me dry. Opening my eyes, I bring my gaze back to her as I thrust into her, harder, faster, feeding off the complete control I have over her.

The control she lets me have.

The control she needs me to have.

"Oh, God," she cries as she pulls on the vines keeping her arms restrained. The more she struggles, the deeper they cut, each movement causing a new self-inflicted wound that leaves a trail of blood leaking down her inked arms.

"I said let go." My command sends her into a frenzy, her body convulses beneath me as I thrust up into her hard and deep, her hips crashing against mine as she grinds on my cock, finally giving in to the hunger she's kept hidden. Her pussy clenches tighter along my shaft as she does what she's told and lets go. "That's it, baby, give it to me."

I fix my eyes on her, watching how her body looks as she comes undone. I want to remember this moment. I want to remember how good she looks and feels when she's broken and cumming on my cock.

I want this memory to be what keeps me up at night.

My little nightmare.

I pull the corn from her mouth as her thighs quiver around me. Her orgasm hits her like an explosion, coursing through her body as she cries out and gasps for air. "That's it, baby. You like it when I tell you what to do, don't you? Filthy girl, cumming on my cock while you roll around in the mud. Yeah? You wanted me to plow you in this field, didn't you?" I keep my rhythm, thrusting deep inside her as she rides out her orgasm, each thrust and clench of her tight cunt bringing me closer to my own release.

Women usually think I'm twisted when I get them to bed, none have been able to handle what it takes to get me off. But my girl, she loves this twisted shit as much as I do. She wants to be used. She wants to be filled with my warm cum. It's why she made catching her so easy; she's known since that night at Rustic Roast that she needed me to satisfy her craving. Her addiction. Coming down from her orgasm, her panting slows as her hips meet me with every thrust. She's not fighting anymore, she's seen what I can give her, and now my little nightmare wants more.

Staring down at her exposed flesh, I flick her swollen clit causing her eyes to dilate with a wild hunger for more. I push inside her deeper as I bring my hand between her thighs and rub her clit in circular motions.

Finally, I'm witnessing the show I've been waiting for. I watch as she comes undone, and any shred of fight she had, has been shattered.

She's fucking mine.

Every broken piece of her belongs to me. Her body tenses as she whimpers, and I know she's close to cumming all over my cock again.

"Don't you fucking cum again. Not yet," I command.

Her lust-filled eyes meet mine as she pouts. She grinds her hips against mine, craving more friction to feed the release I have forbidden her from having.

"Hold it. You don't cum until I tell you to," I growl as I pump into her faster, racing to meet her incoming orgasm. I grip her hips tightly, my fingers digging into her flesh as I quicken my pace. Her back arches off the ground and her head falls back into the bloodied dirt.

"Please," she begs. "I can't take it anymore. Please—"

"That's right baby, beg for me. Beg for me to fill you with my cum." I know she's been waiting for it. She wants it, she wants me to claim her.

"Yes- I need it, I can't," she admits with lust in her shaky voice.

I slam into her hard one last time. My balls tighten, and my release hits me.

"Fuck." I hiss. "Cum baby. Come with me like a good girl."

She obeys, squeezing my cock as I fill her with my cum, claiming her. If she had doubts about being mine before, there is no way she will now. She'll never forget me breaking down her walls, how I make her give in to the dark needs she has rooted deep inside her, showing her how to free it.

I slide my slick dick from her folds, causing streams of our mixed fluids to leak out and on to the dry earth as she lifts her flushed face to mine. I run my fingers through her cum filled cunt, coating them in the sweet combination of our releases before dragging them across her swollen lips. She looks at me with disgust, and I can't help but find it funny.

"Oh come on, we both know how much you love pumpkin cream," I add, cocking a mischievous brow.

When I'm finished tucking myself back into my pants, I reach over her head with my blade, cutting her wrists free from the thorny pumpkin vines. With her wrists freed, she quickly goes to cover herself, and I chuckle.

"No point in hiding now, Cara. Every inch of you is mine, and I've seen it all," I whisper, offering her a cocky grin. "Now, let's get you home. I have a surprise for you."

She's confused, unsure of how to feel about what's happened. I expected this. I knew there would be some lingering feelings after I claimed her the way I did. After I ruined her. That's why I have my little surprise waiting for her at home.

She's going to fucking love it.

Chapter Fourteen
CARA

Finding words for what just happened is harder than I could have imagined. My head feels heavy from the effects of the alcohol I consumed tonight, making processing any of it next to impossible. I'm not even sure how to feel about it. How should I feel about the stranger in the pumpkin mask? How should I feel about him chasing me through a field like a predator would chase his prey?

That's what I was tonight, his prey, and I think I fucking loved it.

I liked that he forced me to do horrible things far outside of my comfort zone. I liked riding the line between pleasure and pain, but he also gave me the best sex of my entire life.

Is this my reward for finally deciding to kick Jonah to the curb? Is Rhett a special delivery sent to me by the devil, praising my desire for mind-blowing sex?

Or is Rhett the devil himself?

Either way, my pussy is still throbbing like a starved bitch at a buffet, wanting more of his cock and its metal piercings that somehow managed to strike every sensitive spot inside me, almost as though they were placed there just for me.

"What's wrong, little nightmare?" He whispers as he guides me through the field.

Little nightmare.

That's what he calls me, acting as though I'm the one keeping him up at night. Does he not see the wrong in what he's done? In what we've done? Even if I did somehow find pleasure in it, it was fucked up. All of it. He's fucked up.

I don't respond to his question, keeping my eyes on the ground as I rub at the torn and bruised flesh around my wrists. The contact of my crusty, dirt covered hands rubbing against the open wounds stings, but I find myself unable to stop. That burn is the only thing keeping me from passing out.

"Still having doubts about who you belong to?" he questions from behind the pumpkin mask.

Jonah's mask. His tone is somehow alluring, yet terrifying and I still have no idea how he ended up with Jonah's mask. A mix of feelings overwhelms me as he drags me through the field. His hand digs tightly into the dirty flesh of my arm as he strings me along.

My costume is ruined, covered in a mix of blood, mud and cum. The hair I spent hours doing is matted and filled with crusty pumpkin leaves, among many other things. I cringe at the thought of how disgusting I look after what was just done to me, what was forced on me.

His voice pulls me from my darkening thoughts, "I promise once you see what I've made for you, you'll never doubt us again."

I don't want to see what he's made. I don't care what surprise he has in store for me. I should be fighting and screaming. I want to fight, to break free and run, but I know it's useless. This masked predator isn't going to give up on his prey. He would chase me down again in a heartbeat.

But, perhaps part of me wants him to. I know it should be wrong, but is it? What if it's just two people fucking in public?

I want him to catch me again.

Fuck me. Claim me. Again.

No.

These thoughts are wrong. This man wants to corrupt me. Ruin me.

But, I want to let him. I don't want to think about how it looks, about what others, even Sloan, would say about it. All that matters is how alive I feel when he does it, and how each barrier he knocks down allows me to feel more free, more like myself. I shouldn't feel this way, shouldn't be struggling with the internal battle of confusing emotions, but I can't help it.

It's like I'm in a dream state as we make our way across a gravel path toward where a black bike is hidden behind some thick bushes. He releases his hold on me as he approaches it and grabs a helmet from the seat. His hand brushes away the stray hair from my face before he slides it over my head, gently buckling it under my chin.

When he's done he climbs on and starts up the engine before turning his sights back on me. I could've escaped. I could've run during those few split seconds, but I didn't. How did he know I wouldn't run?

"Get on, Cara. I have something to show you."

My knees grow weak at the use of my name departing from his lips. A lump forms in my throat as I obey him. The urge to get out of this place is stronger than my fear of him. I climb on behind him and wrap my arms tightly around his waist as his inked hands grip the throttle.

He takes off, racing down the path along the cornfield and past the party. I don't look back. I don't search the crowds for my friends. I don't seek a glimpse of Sloan. After all, even if I found them, they couldn't save me. They couldn't free me from this predatory man, and I'm not sure I want them to.

The ride through the farm roads and into town feels longer than it should. I grip my arms around him tighter, pressing my chest against his toned back, when I realize just how large his frame really is. He's taller than I thought, and well-toned. Through the side peeks I get around his mask, I can see his perfectly chiseled jaw, and though I can't see it, I have no doubt his face is fucking gorgeous. My pussy throbs with the vibrations of his bike, and all I can think about is how badly I'd rather be riding his face right now. How I'd let him break me any way he wanted, as long as he touched me the way only he can touch me.

With his large tatted hands gripping the throttle and his eyes glued on the road ahead, I allow myself to drown in his husky scent as I grip him tighter, afraid the aftershock of the night and the bike's vibrations against my sensitive pussy will have me falling off the side of his bike and into an orgasmic bliss. Everything seems to blur, and time slows as we speed by familiar storefronts and streets littered with trick-or-treaters, lazily making their way back home with bags packed full of sweet treats.

When we pull up to my house, I'm surprised to find the flickering flames of the tiny candles can still be seen in the jack-o'-lanterns along my stairs. I slide off the bike, and the cold cement is a shock to my senses, almost forcing my knees to give out. As if sensing my struggle, Rhett is quick to grab my arm, keeping me from falling to the ground. I lift my eyes to his mask, suddenly curious about the man behind it.

I wish I could look into his eyes.

What would I see staring back at me?

He chuckles, sensing my internal dialogue as he loosens his grip on my arm and unclips the strap on the helmet, slowly lifting it over my head. I smooth my matted hair with my hands as though it will make any difference to how I look.

I don't even know why I care how I look. I shouldn't, but part of me does. Some small part of me likes his eyes on me, and how his gaze makes me feel.

My pulse increases as he turns me around and directs me up the path toward my house. Halfway up the path, I stop, as the realization of this man knowing where I live hits me.

"How— How did you know where I live?" I choke out.

He pauses behind me, and his tone does little to hide the amusement he finds within my question. "I know everything about you, Cara." He explains, tucking a strand of hair behind my ear. "You belong to me, and I take care of what is mine. Protect what is mine."

Feeling even more confused by his words, I slowly continue up the path, but this time he doesn't follow. I turn, looking over my shoulder, and find him standing half way up the path, his hands at his sides as he watches me. His gaze sends a chill up my spine, and I find myself wondering why he stopped, why he didn't follow me right to my door.

My feet are numb from the cold, and I do my best to hurry the rest of the way, up each step of the stairs past dying jack-o'-lanterns. I spent way too much time carving them, but at the time, they seemed worth it. I always pick the most difficult designs, each one testing my patience and steady hand more than the one before.

Reaching the top step, I glance over my shoulder, finding my predator hasn't moved from his spot in the middle of the path, his hands still at his sides as he watches me. It feels like I'm home free. Like somehow, after what was just done to me, I'm home. I survived. I reach inside the tiny pocket of my costume, pulling out my keys as I turn my gaze towards my locked door.

I stiffen.

Beside the large door of my house, is my grandmother's old chair, but it's not the chair that has the contents of my stomach threatening to make a reappearance, it's the head that sits on top of it, carefully carved to fit in with my collection of jack-o'-lanterns.

Jonah's head.

My keys slip from my trembling hand, hitting the wooden deck of my home. My mouth falls open, unable to tear my eyes from the horrific sight before me. Bile rises in the back of my throat as the scent of decay and rich iron hits my nose, forcing me to take a step back.

"Do you like your gift, little nightmare?" his deep voice emanates from behind me, causing me to spin around in a panic.

Behind me I find my predator, maskless as he stalks toward me with a menacing grin.

ABOUT THE AUTHORS

Melissa McSherry

Melissa is a Canadian stay-at-home mom to seven minions and is happily married to a very patient man. When she isn't writing or reading, she is chasing kids, cleaning, or downing her fifth coffee of the day while binge-watching TV or reading. As a writer of dark romance, usually dark fantasy romance, her books always include possessive men, and lots of bloodshed with the added touch of "WTF" moments and spice!

Connect with Melissa on Instagram or TikTok as @pagemastermama

READER FACEBOOK GROUP:
https://www.facebook.com/groups/193386377078157/

Continue to next page…

Dana LeeAnn

Dana was raised in northern Colorado, where she eventually got married and had two children. In 2022 Dana and her family moved to northern Arkansas, where they currently reside on a 50-acre farm. When Dana isn't writing full-time, you can find her gardening or fishing on one of her ponds.

Connect with Dana on Instagram or TikTok as @danaleeannhunt

READER FACEBOOK GROUP:

https://www.facebook.com/groups/1266397124048561/

ACKNOWLEDGMENTS

Thank you from the bottom of our hearts.

To **<u>Rocky</u>**, for being so quick and efficient with your editing skills.

To **<u>Renee,</u>** for being our ROCK throughout the entire editing process and being the best hype girl we could ask for. You have our endless appreciation.

To <u>our</u> **<u>betas and author friends</u>** for always providing us with honest and sincere feedback. We are forever grateful!

To <u>our</u> **<u>ARC readers</u>**, for being the best hype team we could ask for. Your timely reviews make our lives easier. Thank you!

To <u>our</u> **<u>readers</u>**, for keeping us on my toes and giving us the best feedback. Sometimes criticism is hard, but we appreciate it more than you know.

He is my predator, and I am his prey.
Tonight, he is starving for a taste of what's his.

It was Halloween, my favorite time of the year. I had my dream job as a tattoo artist, a loyal best friend, and an ex who happily tended to my needs without complicating our arrangement with feelings.

Everything was going great until Devil's Night when the masked man watched me from the shadows like a *predator* stalking his next meal, and that's what I was: his *prey*.

Like any natural-born predator, he was bloodthirsty, staking his claim to me before I could see the face behind his mask. He wasn't afraid to kill for a bite of what he craved, even if it meant shedding the blood of those closest to me. Once he had a taste, he hungered for more, and the more he needed it, the more I wanted to give it to him.